Violet

BOOK 1 OF D.E.M.O.N. DAUGHTERS

EMMA JO GREGORY

This and That Publishing, LLC

Book Cover by Book Cover Trove

Trunk chapter image created by Labyrinth Book Designs

First edition 2025

e-book ISBN 979-8-9903502-1-2

paperback ISBN 979-8-9903502-3-6

Printed and bound by IngramSpark. Australia: Ingram Content Group AU Pty Ltd, Melbourne, Victoria. US: Lightning Source LLC, La Vergne, Tennessee / Allentown, Pennsylvania / Jackson, Tennessee, United States. UK: Lightning Source UK Ltd, Milton Keynes, United Kingdom. Europe: Lightning Source UK Ltd, with facilities in Germany, France, and Spain. The authorized representative in the European Economic Area is Lightning Source France, 1 Av. Johannes Gutenberg, 78310 Maurepas, France. compliance@lightningsource.fr

To my own sisters:
for the late night story sessions,
the psychology lessons,
the 'read this' and reading it,
This is for us.

"Violet" was originally published as a short story in *T.AL.E.S. of Wondrously Wicked Witches* in 2024. It has since been expanded, and a few little things have changed in the first six chapters. The biggest is the name of Phillip's sister and what was originally an epilogue is now the end of chapter 6. A huge thank you to everyone who purchased and read ToWWW, it was the debut of this series and me as an author and I will always be grateful to Jamie and D.C. for that!

Chapter One

Just when Violet thought she was used to her youngest sister's randomness, she wandered into the kitchen to, "You should check on the house in Mass."

Violet looked at the time on the coffee pot. "Can I at least have a cup of coffee before you drop whatever weird ass dream you just had? It's seven a.m. Why are you even up?" Seven in the morning during the summer was not exactly a time she expected her eighteen-year-old sister to be up.

"Because you need to go check on the house in Mass. Pour me a cup, please," Abigail asked, with the obligatory youngest-child plea in her voice.

Their oldest sister opened the backdoor, coming in with a handful of fresh flowers from their backyard. "Oh, good, you're up. She wouldn't tell me anything before she told you," Patience said cheerfully.

Everyone needed to take the perky wakefulness down a level or three. She none-too-gently placed Abigail's cup before her with a look that clearly said *keep quiet*.

"Okay, I'll make some toast," Patience said, reading the room. She pulled out a vase and put in her mixed bouquet before washing her hands.

"Do I even want to know?" Violet finally asked Abigail, the silence deafening as they all waited.

"I don't know." Abigail shrugged. "But it was definitely about you."

"And you're sure it wasn't just a normal dream?" Violet asked hopefully.

"I don't even know what that is." Abigail looked at her confused. "Anyway, there was this wall completely filled with locks. All different types in rows up and down this wall that went on for some time. I didn't look at all of them. Didn't need to—it wasn't the point. The one I needed was right in front of me. And it was yours."

"My lock. To what?"

Abigail shrugged. "Dunno. But the key is in Massachusetts. And it's fleeting. I don't think it is in Massachusetts for too long—or at least not permanently."

"That's it?" Violet asked confused, looking at Patience. They were used to Abigail's dreams, used to her seeing things a normal person could never conceive.

A gift that had nothing to do with the family curse.

That was one reason they all trusted it. It was also hard not to trust Abigail. Most of the time.

"You want me to go to Massachusetts because of a dream lock. There must be more."

"It has to do with the curse. I don't know if it's a cure, but it is *something*. And whatever it is, it's related to you. So it can only be revealed to you." Abigail shrugged. "Do we have eggs, Patience? I'm thinking of making some scrambled." She walked to the fridge.

Violet just took a sip of her coffee, letting Abigail's dream percolate. Could it be something tied to her family line? The five of them were raised as sisters, considered themselves sisters, and to the outside world were sisters—albeit very diverse ones. Patience and Violet definitely didn't look like the other three with their respective Indian and Indigenous heritage. She couldn't think of a time when any of the women shared blood now that she thought about it.

Get a grip on your thoughts, Vi, she mentally chided. "A wall filled with locks. Different types of locks. What kind of wall? Were you in a hallway? A room? A house?"

"Don't know." Abigail shrugged before beating eggs. "I didn't get any sense of that. It was a white wall, taller than a normal room, but there was maybe eighteen inches of wall on the top and bottom before the rows of locks started."

"Was there a wall behind you?" Violet asked.

"The walls weren't the point, Vi, so I can't tell you. It doesn't work like that."

Violet wondered if Abigail even knew how her gifts worked. None of the rest of them could see the future, so they couldn't help. And whatever rules past generations had figured out were extremely few.

Or not shared with everyone, Violet thought looking at Patience. It wouldn't surprise her if the Neapolis line kept some secrets from the rest of them. Despite the fact secrets were partly what got them into this curse in the first place.

"All right. Locks. One is mine. And how do you know I'm supposed to go to Massachusetts?"

"It feels right. No one has checked on the house in ages, and isn't there an exhibit at the Museum of Fine Arts you wanted to go to?" Abigail pointed out, dishing up eggs for her and Patience knowing Violet never developed a taste for eggs unless they were in something baked.

"I guess I'm going to Boston, then." Violet looked at Patience who just sat, amused, watching all of this. "Laugh it up, she'll have a dream about you one day then guess who'll be laughing."

"Me." Abigail grinned. "Who says I haven't?" She looked at Patience.

"Details!" Violet demanded, but Abigail took her cup and plate to eat outside, muttering about sisters under her breath.

It was a balmy summer morning in Southern California, and with Patience's garden, it would be picturesque and calm—exactly what she liked after a dream so neither sister would go after her.

Violet grabbed a piece of the buttered toast Patience made. "What do you think?"

"That I want to know what she knows about me. As for you, she clearly knows something more, so I'll try to get out of her what she isn't saying. If nothing else, see that exhibit. Let the change of scenery jar those artistic juices."

"Need me to do anything while I'm there?"

"Just let me know what the house needs and any changes in the neighborhood we should know about." Patience shook her head.

"Let me know what you learn," Violet said as she stood. Apparently, she had a trip to pack for.

By packing, she grabbed what clothes spoke to her for a Boston summer, made sure she had enough underwear, and then carefully packed up her paints. The fact she could pop in—literally—if she needed something meant she didn't stress about what she packed.

She was also convinced she would be back in a day or two unless something struck her creative juices. While she didn't doubt Abigail's dream was about her, she had no idea what the hell she was supposed to be looking for.

Patience waited until she had a text from Violet saying she made it to their house in Swampscott. Moving from one house to the next across the country was as effortless as breathing and happened between one heartbeat and the next. The fact Violet texted she arrived made Patience smile. Now to crack the nut that was their baby sister.

"I'm going to change for work," Patience told Abigail, who was loading her plate into the dishwasher. "What didn't you say?"

"*Moi?*" Abigail said with fake innocence. "How do you know?"

"Eldest sister intuition."

Abigail sighed as she leaned against the counter, crossing her arms across her chest. "She doesn't want to know. That I'm sure of. She'd hide in her room for the rest of her life, literally."

"Doesn't mean I don't want to know. What's this trip really about?" Patience asked, her curiosity ratcheted up an extra notch now.

"This sounds dumb. I am aware of that, so you don't need to tell me. It's a guy."

"A guy?"

"*Her* guy."

"Her... *Oh*." Realization dawned on Patience.

"There was so much potential, and he was just... Is lovely too cringe?" Abigail wondered. "I really liked what I felt around him. But if I told her a guy was involved—"

"She'd hide in her room for the rest of her life, literally." Patience sighed. "Her one goal in life is to not fall in love." The damn curse reared its ugly head, again. "I won't tell her anything but tell *me* anything else that can help her." She knew why Violet would run away from a romantic interest. How many late nights had they stayed up talking about their future love lives? At least Violet's ended happily—if she allowed it.

Abigail grinned impishly. "You enjoy this too much."

"Who doesn't want a happy ending? Let's get it for her. Lord knows she'll need the push." Patience laughed as she went to her room to change into real clothes. She worked from home, but, in her mind, that didn't mean slacking off with schedules or outfits.

Chapter Two

Violet had no idea what she was supposed to do regarding Abigail's dream, so she focused on the house. Her clothes flew into the dresser and closet while she gently unpacked her paints.

A girl had her priorities, after all.

Since she hadn't been to the house in years, she decided to reacquaint herself with it. She had appeared in one of the bedrooms on the second floor of the house—the first image that came to mind with this house. The room itself was not personalized, unsurprising since none of them lived there. She went to the large windows, and even if the room was bland with only a bed, dresser, and vanity, the view of the Atlantic Ocean was gorgeous.

"Note to self, be up for sunrise so you can paint it," she whispered. It would have to be even more wonderous with the sun rising over the horizon.

She went through the jack-and-jill bathroom, checking to make sure there were no leaks anywhere, and into the next bedroom. "Did Patience hire a cleaner?" Violet muttered to herself. It was clear no one lived here, but it was also spotless.

Five bedrooms on this floor and not a speck of dust.

She decided to go upstairs first. The attic was a treasure trove of memories. Half was walled off to create a bedroom and she found dolls, Barbies, and their dress-up chest in it.

"Hello, Andy." Violet smiled as she grabbed the raggedy doll. A memory of how they forced Faith, their second youngest sister, to marry the doll when she was four came to mind, making Violet laugh.

She only gave the other half of the attic a cursory look, not wanting to see what her mother, grandmother, or anyone else may have left there.

She pulled out her cell phone as she walked to the first floor. "Do you secretly pop in once every two weeks to dust?" she asked Patience.

"Hell, no. I hired a cleaner. I take it everything is okay?"

"Haven't met the neighbors, but the house seems great. I found the old Raggedy Andy doll."

"That we forced Faith to marry?" Patience laughed.

"Anything from Abby?" She needed more from the dream to go off.

"No, sorry."

"What am I supposed to go off, Patience?" Violet sighed as she reached the screened-off porch on the back of the house with a view of the Atlantic. It opened into a tiered garden that went down to a rock wall, beyond which was the path to the beach. "And if you say 'just vibes' I will pop back in to punch you."

"That's all I got. Specifically, that's all Abby has. So why not do what you would do if this was a trip for you and see what happens? Maybe Abby will have another dream with more directions tonight or tomorrow."

"I mean, yeah, I'll go to the museum tomorrow. I'm not complaining, but what am I looking for? Am I supposed to look at locks till I find an interesting one? Why on earth did I just pop across the country on a whim?"

"You know it's not a whim. If Abby says something is there for you to find, there is something there. Start with places that speak to you specifically. Which, let's face it, an exhibit of women of the rococo period doesn't speak to any of the rest of us."

"Let me know anything else Abby tells you." Violet sighed. "I know you have to work."

"Of course. Enjoy yourself. When was the last time you were in the North Shore?" Patience pointed out before hanging up.

Wednesday morning, she found herself at the Boston Museum of Fine Arts right as it opened. She could spend the whole day there, so she wanted to get in early.

"Jim!" A mother's voice made everyone in the vicinity stop.

"I'm sorry," a young boy said apologetically.

"Pick up all the pieces." The woman sighed. Violet saw he somehow broke the handheld fan—which honestly, in this heat was a brilliant idea.

"Can I help?" Violet asked.

"They're cheap. He's not in trouble," the woman said quickly.

"Oh, I meant about the fan. I'm good at fixing things," Violet said easily. "In fact..." She reached into her purse and pulled out an identical fan she materialized out of thin air. She leaned down to the boy. "Can I trade you? And I'll fix the other one."

"But it's broken," the boy said in disbelief.

"For now. Give me a few minutes with it." Violet winked, took the broken pieces from him, and gave him the one she magicked.

"Really, that's too kind."

"Not at all. I forgot how muggy it gets in Boston," Violet promised. "Enjoy."

She walked into the next room when a man about her age stopped her.

"That was really sweet," he said, nodding toward the kid.

"Uh, thanks."

"Are you here for the religious art exhibit?"

"No, the other one," Violet said quickly but took him in. Mr. Tall Dark and Handsome looked like Clark Kent with chestnut brown hair. Mr. All-American but nerdy—a combination she never thought about but decided it was delicious. At her five foot eight, she knew he was close to six feet tall, maybe an inch over.

"I admit I don't know about the rococo period. Or to be honest, anything other than the fact it is after the baroque period, and there's a famous portrait of a *Girl Reading a Book*. I think that's what it's called. My sister loves that painting."

Violet raised an eyebrow, amazed he even knew anything about the rococo period. "It's 'A Young Girl Reading', or *La Liseuse*. It won't be in the exhibit since it was painted by a man. Why are you interested in the religious exhibit?"

"It speaks to me easier," he admitted, and she felt like he was being genuine. "Grew up in the Church. It reminds me of my childhood."

"That's... Sorry, never mind. I hope you enjoy the exhibit," she said, mentally kicking herself.

She nearly got lost in his eyes and almost asked him for more information to keep the conversation going before she caught herself. *What are you doing, Vi?* She mentally chided. She was thinking he had warm, chocolate brown eyes that looked kind and incapable of deceit.

Danger, Will Robinson! Warning sirens went off in her head. It had been, well, years since she found a man attractive who wasn't dead, in a painting, or a celebrity. She was content with that. She was purposely sticking to that. *Did you forget the alternative*? If she had a way of mentally slapping herself with her power, she would have done it.

"Actually," he said quickly when she turned toward her exhibit. "I'm a historian. Well, historian in the making. I'm working on my doctorate. Which is a really long-winded way of saying I like learning. Especially about history stuff. So this looks like an opportunity to learn. Like I said, I don't know much about the rococo period. Apparently not even the name of my sister's favorite painting, and now I'm rambling," he blushed.

"It is perfectly fine to not enjoy all pieces of art," Violet pointed out. *Focus on the art, Vi,* she told herself. Art was safe, she couldn't get in trouble talking about art. This nerd, she was learning quickly with his blushes and rambling, not safe.

"Even in the same period, I find myself more drawn towards certain artists than others."

"Completely. I mean, I know. What failed to come out was I would like to tour the exhibit. Learn. If you don't mind."

"I couldn't stop you," Violet lied. She absolutely could and wouldn't hesitate to use her power if need be. They learned long ago that a handful of spectators could be blocked from seeing something they did, especially in a confined area like a room in a museum.

But he was giving off nerdy Clark Kent vibes, and she had serious doubts he meant her harm.

"I promise not to pester you with too many questions." He grinned, and damn it, it was cute. His grin reached his eyes, and she realized they were lighter than she first realized, more like honey chocolate. *What is with these thoughts, Violet?*

"Bold proposition. I don't even know your name," she pointed out, and he blushed so deep she worried he'd be dehydrated soon if they kept talking.

"I'm mortified. My mother raised me better, I promise. I'm Phillip."

"Violet. I'll give you five questions. Make them count." She smiled, and his returning smile lit up his countenance in a way she wanted to paint.

The first pieces in the exhibit hall were portraits of Marie Antoinette by Elisabeth Vigge Le Brun.

"I know these," Phillip said, studying them. "I never thought of them as from the rococo period. Then again, I was more interested in the aftermath of the French Revolution."

"Do you study the French Revolution?" she wondered. He said he was a historian.

"Do you get five questions too?" he teased, and she laughed. "No. I've taken classes on it. We have someone on faculty who teaches an amazing class on it. It's a fascinating period. Nasty," he quickly clarified seeing her lack of a reaction, not sure how to take it. "But so many things happened in such a short period of time. We see the capacity for violence and human inventiveness. Yet in the end, it fails."

"At a horrible price," Violet pointed out.

"Of course," he said as they moved on. He asked about something he noticed about the paintings, and she was impressed with the fact he was actually studying the paintings. She wasn't completely clueless and knew he asked because he was interested, but the fact he was also taking this seriously made her smile.

He was a nerd, and she found herself attracted to it. Who knew?

"So the exhibit is to showcase a new piece," he said looking at the placard on display. "Something by Rose-Adélaïde Ducreux. How did they know it was hers if she never signed her work? Also, why *wouldn't* you sign your work? Especially if you knew men would lay claim to it?" he asked, puzzled.

"That's two questions," Violet pointed out. "As for the first, new technology reveals lots of things. As for why she didn't sign, I have no idea. I can't imagine not signing my work. A signature can be more than just a scribble of a name if you want it to be part of the larger picture."

"You're an artist." He smiled. "I must have sounded like an imbecile. Would I have seen your work?"

"Probably not. And you didn't," she promised. "It makes me sad she didn't. It was such an accomplishment for women to finally be on the art scene as artists. Why she didn't claim ownership of her work puzzles me," Violet pursed her lips as she studied the new portrait.

"I know you only came to see this exhibit, but would you like to tour the other one?" Phillip asked cautiously, eagerly.

"Are you going to explain it to me?" she teased.

"I wouldn't dare. My sister made sure I knew when I mansplained growing up. I'm also smart enough to know when I'm the expert in the room and humble enough to admit it isn't now."

Okay, she could understand why people would swoon. Nerdy *and* humble? She had to get out of here and was about to make an excuse but realized it was driven by fear. Instead she excused herself to find the bathroom and splashed water on her face.

She looked at her reflection in the mirror above the sink. "Get a grip, Vi. Enjoy someone being interested in you." She couldn't remember the last time she found herself in this situation. "Enjoy yourself. It's just the museum with a cute nerd. A nerd is not a lock, stop being an idiot."

A nerd was not a lock, but perhaps he was more of a guide? Could there be something in the other exhibit? The museum was definitely her thing, as Patience pointed out. She had to at least look everywhere.

She found him outside the other exhibit, and he was visibly relieved when she joined him. "I'll be honest and say I thought you might have ditched me, that I might have come on too strong."

"Were you coming onto me?" Violet smiled as she passed him to go inside.

He grinned as he followed her in.

They were nearly at the end when she jumped, shocked. A lock. Ever so small in the painting before her.

"Do you know this piece?" she asked Phillip.

"No. It's newer. This is the part that highlights New England artists of the last fifty years," he told her.

She snapped a photo of the plaque describing the piece and the artist. She would have to come back and look at it when the museum was closed to see if it was anything more than a painting but *holy shit*.

"I enjoyed that more than I expected," Violet said honestly. "I'm not religious. My youngest sister is. But I learned a lot," she admitted as they exited.

A food truck was parked down the block, and Phillip looked back at her as she put on some sunglasses. "Can I treat you to lunch? Are you vegan?" he asked worriedly.

"I think of myself as an omnivore." Violet smiled.

"Let me buy you lunch, then. It is the least I can do after you put up with me."

"It wasn't a chore," Violet promised and realized she had enjoyed herself.

They got a table as they waited for the food. "I have two questions left." Phillip smiled.

"Two?"

"You technically couldn't answer one of them." He grinned mischievously. "So it shouldn't count. You mentioned a sister?" he asked.

"I have four," Violet said, and he raised an eyebrow.

"I grew up with one. I love her to death, but I can't imagine having four."

"Is it just the two of you?" He nodded and she wondered what it was like to be such a normal family. "I can't imagine any differently. I love them, even when they drive me crazy." Like sending her across the country to find a lock.

"One older sister was enough."

Violet grinned. "Patience is ours. She is an absolute saint—which sucks."

He laughed. "I think it's the eldest girl curse."

Her laugh faltered for just a moment at the mention of 'curse' and she hoped he didn't notice. "So, grad student. Are you doing it here in Boston?" She knew from earlier he was from Boston even though his accent was very faint.

"That would make sense given my thesis, but no. I wanted to get away. I love my family but wanted to live somewhere else. At least for a while. Turns out, I can't shake my sister that easily, she works in the same city practically now. My parents, thankfully, still live here in Boston. Gives me an excuse to come home and live rent-free while I do field work."

"Field work?"

"Looking through some archives here in the city and some further north."

"That means nothing to me." Violet laughed. They had finished eating but she had no desire to leave anytime soon. "I didn't go to college," Violet admitted.

"Art school?" he asked but she shook her head.

Suddenly, she felt so dumb next to him. How must she look? He was getting his PhD for crying out loud. A little overwhelmed and starting to feel the humidity, she pulled out the kid's fan from her bag she'd reassembled with a spritz of her powers.

"You really fixed it?" Phillip asked, shocked, seeing her use the fan.

"That's your last question," she pointed out, torn between not wanting to leave and wanting a giant hole to open and swallow her.

"I withdraw it," he said immediately and she felt the corners of her mouth twitch in amusement. "Instead, I'll ask if I can see you again."

"Really?"

He grinned.

Now, she was blushing. "I'm not sure how long I'll be in Boston. I mean, technically I'm on the North Shore. I popped in for a day trip."

He took out a business card—*a business card*—and scribbled a number on it. "Here's my cell. I'm here for at least the rest of the month. What part of the North Shore?"

"Swampscott."

"I would like to see you again," he said honestly. "I'll be up in Salem day after tomorrow, actually. Can I buy you lunch?"

"Salem." She sighed. "Nothing touristy," she said, and he crossed his heart. "If I call you," she amended as she stood. "I have to get to something. Thanks for lunch, Phillip," she said sincerely.

"I hope you call, Violet."

Chapter Three

Violet popped into Patience's home office with a glare that would have killed lesser mortals. She dropped into a chair opposite Patience who was watching something on her computer.

"This was unexpected." Patience looked up from her screens, muting the finance news show she had on.

"Tell me Abigail did not send me to Boston for a boy."

"Why would she send you for a boy?"

"Man, whatever. You know what I mean!" she shouted, the force of her frustration driving her to her feet.

Patience looked at her confused. "What is going on?"

Violet let out a noise somewhere between a scream and a cry of frustration, throwing her arms around as she vented. "I went to the museum, and there was a boy. An actual boy. I helped him, and then this man sideswiped me. And next thing I know, we're touring the museum together and having lunch, and he wants to see me again. Did Abigail see this?" she demanded.

"Why are you asking me?" Patience pointed out. "I'm not the one with prophetic dreams. She went out with Faith. Call her," Patience told her, naming their fourth and the second youngest sister.

"She would have told you." Everyone told Patience everything. Even if they didn't, she somehow still knew everything—eldest sister intuition, apparently.

"I've been in here following these French companies I've had an eye on for a while. Things are about to dip like I've been waiting for," Patience said triumphantly.

"I don't want to know. He's working on his PhD," Violet said as she took a seat again, defeated.

"So?" Patience asked confused.

"I never went to college. Or art school. Nothing. I'm a dumb dumb in comparison."

"First, why do you care suddenly?" Patience pointed out. "It's never bothered you before. It was a choice you made. It was right for you."

"I know. Why would someone so educated want a second date with me?" Violet wondered.

Patience raised an eyebrow before looking at something on her screen. She typed for several minutes before letting out a "yes" and shifting her attention back to Violet. "Did this guy say anything that made you feel dumb?" she wondered.

"No," Violet sighed.

"Then why are you making a big deal out of it?" Patience asked.

At that, Violet had no response. "I found a lock," she said shifting gears.

"What? Where?"

"In the museum. I'm going to go in tonight. Want to come with?"

"In case you open a demon portal like a television show? Yes, ma'am. Now let me work."

Violet saluted and popped back into the bedroom in Swampscott. She was going to research the artist and painting before they went in that night.

"This is exciting!" Hannah said doing a happy dance when she and Patience arrived in the living room. Their middle sister looked around, her pale red hair bouncing around in loose ringlets in her excitement. "I forgot how much I liked this house," she added. "It has the second-best music room after our home," she added.

"We're busting into a museum after hours and you're thinking about music rooms." Patience rolled her eyes.

Hannah's grin gave off "happy to be here" vibes, making Violet laugh. At twenty, she managed to pull off the fairy, otherworldly look effortlessly.

"Why are you here?" Violet wondered.

"Patience said she wanted backup. What are the odds we open a demon gate?"

"Minimal," Patience decided. "But just in case."

"Faith seems more like the demon gate type," Hannah pointed out.

"Probably, but you are more sneak-into-places-middle-of-the-night," Patience decided. "You are more of a fairy ninja. Faith would have a shootout with a demon at high noon without batting an eyelash."

"Facts," Hannah decided.

"Are we ready?" Violet asked. "Let's see what this is about. Hopefully, it will reveal whatever Abigail dreamed about and this will be over." Then she wouldn't have to think about Phillip's offer for a second date.

They appeared in the wing in front of the painting a moment later. They had a dusting of their power pulsing over them like a second skin—something they realized would keep cameras and videos from capturing their image or set of motion detectors.

"Oh, I see it," Hannah said, finding the small lock on the canvas.

With her hands covered in power like a pair of gloves, Violet pulled the painting off the wall, the alarm dead. She looked it over, front and back. She tried touching the lock. Nothing.

"Can I see?" Patience asked and took the painting Violet passed her.

"Well, no demon." Hannah looked around.

"You say that matter of factly. Faith would be disappointed." Violet laughed.

"Well, it's a nice painting." Patience shrugged handing it back.

"I don't know what I expected to happen. Maybe the lock unlocking in the painting or something." Violet sighed. "Should I bring the painting to Abby?"

"She said in the dream the lock unlocked when you touched it. So if nothing happened, this isn't it," Patience decided.

Well, shit. Now what was she going to do?

"Hey, now you can go on a date with a cute nerd. I looked him up." Patience grinned, and Hannah smiled.

"He's so cute! I can feel the nerd vibes from his social media." Hannah agreed.

"Are there no secrets?" Violet wondered.

Patience and Hannah both chimed, "Nope."

Patience materialized back in their home. Hannah decided to spend the night in Swampscott with Violet. She wanted to see if the baby grand piano was in tune and have a go on it.

"Well?" Abigail asked when she found Patience.

"She's resisting."

"And you think Hannah is the one to get her to go out with him again?"

"She has a better chance than Faith. Or you. Faith would reinforce everything Vi fears, she's too suspicious of you at the moment. Hannah thinks it's cute and will make it seem like an adventure. She understands the mission," Patience promised. The fact Violet brought up Phillip before the key she found in the painting was a good sign in her mind.

Chapter Four

Phillip brought up the profile page for Violet. Like most, there wasn't a lot that was public, but her banner photo was a recent family photo of six girls celebrating the one in the middle in graduation robes. There she was on one side. He guessed the other Indigenous girl in the center of the photo in a graduation robe was one of her sisters. They were both tall, native girls with dark hair, dark eyes, and similar facial features. Beyond that, he had no idea. She said she had four sisters, but the family in the photo looked nothing alike. Three of the girls were white but had very different shades of eyes and hair. On the other side of the group, the oldest was a woman he guessed was Indian.

His sister cleared her throat, bringing him back to the moment. "Why call if you're going to ignore me?"

"Maybe I don't want to know what you have to say, Colleen."

"I don't hear anything wrong. I mean, not introducing yourself could have been cute or creepy. I wasn't there."

"I can hear you smirking over the phone you know." He sighed. "I can't explain it. It was a kick in the gut when I saw her."

"My scientifically minded brother is describing love at first sight. I love it." She laughed. "In all seriousness, I don't think you did anything, and I'm hoping she calls you because I kind of like my serious, nerdy brother being thrown for a loop."

"I thought older sisters were supposed to be protective?"

"Oh, I'll kick her ass if I need to. In the meantime, I'm hoping for entertainment."

"Next time I call, don't pick up," Phillip decided. He heard a text and checked his phone.

"Was it her?" Colleen asked excitedly. "Hello? You there? Answer me!"

"Where can I take her in Salem? Nothing too touristy."

"Why are you going to Salem?" she demanded.

"I got access to an archive..." he hedged.

"I'll ask some friends. I saw a new café opened. Even if working her in around your schedule is far from romantic. I'll text you some recommendations. You ask her which she would like to meet you at. Narrow it down to two," Colleen ordered. "Let me reach out to friends. You got this! Love you." She cheered him on before hanging up.

"Oh, I like the look of this one," Hannah said from where she was lounging on one of the sofas opposite Violet. "Cute, decent menu, good ratings."

"What the hell am I doing?" Violet shook her head and texted him her choice.

"You are going on a casual lunch date with a man you won't see again once you leave Boston. Where's the harm in that? You're allowed to have fun, Vi. Besides, you found one lock with him. It wasn't the right one, but it was hardly going to be the first thing you found."

Violet twirled Phillip's business card in her hand. Doctoral Candidate at UCLA. He was doing his degree half an hour from her home. She told herself Los Angeles was home to over three million people. The odds of running into him again were very slim, even with Faith and soon her cousin going to the university.

"True. But I still have nothing to go on. Am I looking for a physical lock? A door with an interesting lock? A locksmith?"

Hannah rolled over to look at her. "I don't know, and I don't know if Abby knows. What I know is it is tied to your line. Maybe something historical? A historian might come in handy, then."

Violet studied her, thoughtfully. "I haven't thought of that. I don't even know what he studies." Not the French Revolution or art.

"So you'll have something to talk about. Just be yourself."

Be herself without revealing anything actually about herself. Yeah, easy peasy.

She set an alarm to be up at sunrise. She was tired, but the view was absolutely worth it as she first took some photographs to capture the first rays of sun on the Atlantic. She had her paints set up in the backyard's outdoor lounge area, and she set a second alarm on her phone so she wouldn't lose track of time and be late.

About an hour before she was going to shower for what she decidedly was not thinking of as a date, she heard piano notes. Hannah was testing the piano, and for the next hour, she relaxed, listening to a variety of Mozart and Chopin.

It was like stepping back in time, hearing it. She could almost hear her mother and Patience's mother talking over a cup of coffee in the closed-in porch.

It was suddenly too much, so she cleaned up her station and went to shower.

The café was filled with a late lunch rush, but she spotted Phillip easily at a table.

"I hear the food is great, and it is definitely cute." Violet smiled as he pulled her seat out for her.

Nerd, smart, *and* a gentleman? Shit.

"My sister recommended it. I haven't been up here for a while."

"So far so good." Violet smiled. She knew what she wanted since she already looked at the menu, so they got their order in.

"Besides art and history, what are you into?" she asked.

"Well, I'm about to start a new job so that has taken up a lot of my time," he admitted. "Going to baseball games comes from my dad. Lots of great memories of us at Fenway over the years." He gave her a boyish grin and she could see him decked out in Red Sox gear.

"My dad was more of a basketball guy. Lakers were his team, but he did appreciate the Celtics."

"So Angels or Dodgers?" Phillip asked. He heard "was" and worried he hit a sore spot.

"Dodgers." She grinned. They talked about sports, and he surprised her mentioning his sister was an amateur photographer. "So art is in your family, too."

"Not with me," Phillip promised. "I'm the academic, or as she likes to accuse me of, the science one. My talent begins and ends with stick figures."

"Nothing wrong with that," Violet said. "Patience loves numbers. Makes me sick to my stomach, personally, but she watches stock markets all day and loves all things economics. Yet she also gardens."

"She's the oldest?" Phillip asked, and Violet nodded.

He paid when they finished, and they decided to stretch their legs.

"You said 'was' with your father," he brought up. "I'm sorry if you lost him."

"Thanks. Both of my parents died when I was a teenager," she admitted. "So Patience really was both big sister and maternal figure. My aunt was there, so we had family. We stayed a family."

"I can't imagine," he said surprised.

"My turn to ask you a personal question," she decided. "But first, ice cream." She nodded toward the parlor.

"I thought you said nothing touristy?"

"Does not apply to ice cream," she declared as he opened the door for her to the retro '50s ice cream parlor. "So," she decided as they continued their walk with ice cream cones, "you were at the archives this morning?"

"And afternoon. Possibly the rest of the week. Mostly hoping to find something but I know realistically it's a stretch."

"That means nothing to me." She laughed.

"I'm trying to find more evidence for my dissertation. My adviser won't let me progress further without it, which I understand. I want there to be more, but if I can't find it, I'll have to go with plan B. I tell myself I can continue after the diss if I have to."

"So what is this mysterious dissertation on? All I know is it's in history."

"I found an obscure reference to a witch trial after the Salem trials. I want to find more— Are you okay?"

She didn't know you could choke on ice cream till now. She took a long drink of the water he offered. "Wrong pipe," she choked out. "Sorry. A witch trial after Salem? I didn't think there was one."

"Most don't, hence obscure. If this is boring or offensive, we can talk about something else." His family didn't get it either. He knew most people didn't understand what doing a dissertation was like and was okay with that.

"Not boring at all," she promised. "Tell me more."

"Well, there's a newspaper article from a Salem paper dated about a decade after the Salem Witch trials. The only other documentation I can find is an old letter saying to beware the demon daughters."

"Holy shit," Violet said.

"Crazy, right?" He grinned. "I know it's unusual for a guy to care about witch trials. I can't explain it. It wasn't what I planned to study."

"So how did you get to this?"

"I took my adviser's class. She connects witch trials across the US and England. It just struck me as fascinating. I can't explain it. I went down a rabbit hole. Last summer, I was trying to figure out what to do my dissertation on and was in the library archives when I came across the letter."

"Here in Boston?" *Note to self, find said letter and burn after reading.*

"Yeah. I haven't been up the North Shore in ages," he said between licks of his ice cream. "Want to go to the beach?"

"How about tomorrow?" She needed to plan a break-in at the library archives.

Chapter Five

Violet put all thoughts of why she was eager for a trip to the beach out of her head. Patience brought Faith in for their library search, who, after grumbling about having the boring job, found the letter in under an hour.

You're doing this for more information, she told herself.

"Hi," she greeted Phillip when he arrived at their house.

"No one lives here full time?" he wondered. It was a stately Georgian colonial on the edge of the town. Behind this street the homes had a gorgeous view of the Atlantic and a private beach.

"No, a great-great-grandmother bought it on principle," Violet explained. "Long story. We had lovely autumns here."

"Where's home?"

"Southern California," she said. "Garage is this way." She had materialized her car from home that first day to run to the grocery store. She offered to drive—she enjoyed it—and he was using the trains while in town for the summer.

"When was the last time you were at the beach?" she asked him as they drove along the shoreline.

He thought about it. "High school? You?"

"Probably about the same," she said.

"Don't repeat this on this coast, but I find I prefer the Pacific." Phillip grinned.

"They'd crucify you out here," she said with faux shock. "I'm a SoCal girl at heart, but the last few mornings I spent painting the ocean view from the house. I forgot how wonderful it is."

Conversation was easy on the drive up to Rockport with a playlist of Nora Jones and Jewel quietly playing.

"I found your social media," he told her and grinned apologetically at the look she gave him.

"My sisters apparently found yours, so I guess we're even."

"You didn't cyber stalk me?" he asked wounded.

She laughed. "I have four sisters to suss out any information that's out there."

"That's fair. My sister found your artist page and loves your work now," he said. He was also a fan but didn't mention it. Was he coming on too strong?

"If she has a site with her photographs I'd love to see it. I've been busy so I haven't had a chance to look for her work yet."

"She does mostly commercial things and set work for films."

"Anything I'd have seen? I have a sister that does scene doubling when they need a pianist."

"Really? Which sister?"

"Hannah. If you saw photos, she is the redhead." She gave him a look as she parked. "We're diverse, I know."

"It must have been your sister's graduation photo I saw. She was in the robes."

"My sister and cousin both graduated this year. If it's the photo I'm thinking of, that would have been my cousin." Leaning over the top of the car after they parked, she smiled seeing him unsure how to approach his question. "We're sisters but have different dads. We know we don't look alike," she said easily giving him half the truth. "Doesn't matter to us. I couldn't love them anymore if we shared parents."

Weeks flew by where she spent most of her days either talking with Phillip when he wasn't in archives or painting and sketching. They acted like tourists, going to different sites around the North Shore, and twice more, she found a lock that turned out to be a dead end.

Yet Abigail swore she was close.

Nothing made sense anymore. "Maybe I need to create it?" she thought aloud. She was the artist of the family, and after several weeks, she had nothing to show for her search.

She opened to a blank page in her sketchbook and said softly, "What would a lock that speaks to me look like?" She would draw what spoke to her. Then if nothing happened, she'd get a description from Abigail of the dream lock.

A week into her attempts to draw the lock into existence yielded nothing. "I give up. No locks, not today," Violet yelled into the universe. She grabbed the beach chair from the shed, her sketch pad, and her water and took the path behind their house the neighbors used to get to the little private beach.

Violet scoped it out after setting her stuff down. "Definitely prefer the Pacific," she said. Something about the Atlantic seemed colder and smelled fishier. Which made her think of Phillip. He had said something similar on one of their outings.

She settled in to sketch the view. An hour later, she jumped when the man of her musings appeared. "Phillip? What are you doing here?"

"You didn't answer the door. And your car was in the garage. I decided to give this a try."

"Did you call and I missed it?" Violet grabbed her phone to check.

"No. I thought about it, but thought it was best to talk to you in person."

"That sounds ominous."

He grinned and leaned against the post where the trail opened onto the beach. "I can't explain it, but for the last several weeks, I've been obsessed with two things. First was finding something to support my dissertation, which makes sense because it's what I planned to spend my summer doing. But it almost started to feel personal, the need to find out more about this particular witch hunt started to consume me. I almost skipped the museum because of it. If I had, I wouldn't have met you. My second obsession."

"Phillip," Violet warned, standing.

"I don't mean psycho-stalker type," he promised, holding his hands up. "Which, I already confessed to cyberstalking you. That's normal for this era, right?" He asked, rubbing one hand on his jean-clad leg. "I mean, I think about you when I haven't talked to you. I hate talking on the phone, but I love hearing your voice. I find I don't care if I don't get in as many hours as I would like going through archives if I'm spending that time with you."

"Phillip, we just met. I have no interest in a long-term relationship."

"Why? The distance? My job starts next month back in SoCal. I know the traffic sucks but depending on where you are, we're talking an hour or two, not across the country."

"I don't even know what this job is."

"Teaching high school history."

"It's not personal. I just don't have any interest in being in a relationship."

"I hear no. I do," Phillip insisted. "I also see you're scared. Of me?" The thought he somehow frightened her made him sick to his stomach.

"No!" she said quickly. "It's hard to explain. Let's say there's a family curse, and it doesn't end well."

She fully expected him to roll his eyes and decide *yup, this girl is crazy*. He was an academic, a scientist, and here she was throwing out the opposite of all of that.

He didn't run for the hills, and she figured he just didn't believe her.

"I felt this itch to go back to the beginning." The change in conversation threw her for a second. "So as soon as the archives opened, I went to find the letter that started it all. A letter from Nathaniel Lorn to Benjamin Smithe warning him to beware the demon daughters. It's nowhere to be found. The archivist actually thought for a minute I snatched it and was playing confused to keep the document."

"Well, they didn't lock you up," Violet observed.

He grinned, and she fought against her heart because that upside down smile was just perfection, making him look both angelic and devilish at the same time. "No one has been in to look in that box for some time, so they're going to look through everything. What I can't figure out is if it's not there, where it could have gone. It's a random reference between two men over three hundred years ago, seemingly saying something disparaging about women."

"I'm sure things get lost all the time."

"Not really. Archivists take their job seriously. Then I remembered my cyberstalking, Violet Exeter."

She didn't like the way he said her name as if he found a secret key to unlock a treasure. "I never hid my name. In fact, it's fairly easy to find since I want people to find my art."

"Yes. Your sisters were difficult since we're not connected on socials: Patience Dubrovnik, Hannah Milan, Faith Orleans, and Abigail Neapolis. If it wasn't in age order, I maybe wouldn't have seen it right away, but this crazy idea popped into my head. Demon isn't a misogynistic reference to women. It refers to specific women: D-E-M-O-N. Tell me I'm wrong."

"Our last names spell 'demon.' Can't deny that."

"You know what I mean, Vi. Be honest. I know you're not being honest about how you feel."

"It's called a crush, Phillip. We barely know each other."

"Then why are you scared of it?" he wondered. "If it's all flash and burn, it will be over soon."

Because she was terrified it wasn't flash and burn and would end in absolute heartbreak. Which would be entirely her fault.

"You're right, allow me to demonstrate," Violet said. Her eyes went completely white and suddenly a second beach chair appeared in front of him. "Is this what you had in mind?" She gestured to her things which disappeared right before his eyes. "Or would you prefer something more biblical?" she asked and walked the short distance to the beach, the water splitting at her feet to create a small path for her to walk on. She turned around after walking about fifteen feet into the now divided ocean, expecting to see him running back up to the main road.

"I have no idea what I expected. This wasn't it," he admitted and tentatively walked after her. She just stared at him in shock.

"You are insane!"

"Probably." He grinned. "I'll admit the eyes shocked me. I did nothing but think about it last night. I'm operating on a triple shot. Because there is no way this could be real. They burned women, not witches. Witches aren't real. And yet, here I stand." He gestured.

"You are crazy." Violet shook her head.

"For you." He smiled, and she rolled her eyes. The fact they were still all white as she did so was disturbing, but he couldn't bring himself to look away so he noticed a tiny burst of gold where the center of her retinas should have been.

"If witches are real—" he started, but she cut him off.

"We don't use that word. It isn't magic wands and potions and stuff."

"Do you have a different word?"

They were standing on the ocean floor bed with water parted up to her knees on either side of the aisle she created. And they were discussing semantics.

"This is getting weird even for me." She shook her head, the water crashing around their feet as she walked back to the beach.

He caught up with her. "Whatever you call it. Anyone with abilities could avoid witch trials. But this group of families were singled out. Why?"

"How long do you have?" she drawled.

He stood in front of her between her and the path. "As long as it takes. I want to know you, Violet. All parts of you, and this is a major part."

"This is the part where you go running for the hills, screaming *the witch is after me,* and I have to stop you." She shook her head.

"I mean, I don't mind running if you're the one chasing me." He smirked.

"What is with you?" Violet asked perplexed. "Do you have a death wish?"

"You won't hurt me."

"I wouldn't be so sure about that," she warned. "We don't have any name for it. We just talk about our 'powers' or 'abilities.' And keep them to ourselves."

"Is your aunt also one?"

"She is an in-law. She's amazing but completely human."

"So it's just you and your four sisters? A matriarchically magic line. Sorry, not magic," he caught himself.

"For us. There are others."

"My head is screaming at me to take notes. Not to share with the world," he added quickly. "Just to remember the details. Can you sketch us in the water?" he asked bewildered, thrilled.

"You'll die."

"What?"

"My line. I told you there was a curse."

"I thought it was hyperbolic."

"I wish." Violet folded her arms across her chest as she stared at him. "My line falls in love, but their lover dies. Every single time."

"This is screaming a movie my sister loved growing up."

"My father was the most recent. June 2 of the woman's thirty-fifth year of life. My grandfather, great-grandfather, and three times great-grandfather—there wasn't a great-great in the picture. Each died on June 2 of the woman's thirty-fifth year of life. I'm twenty-five, Phillip. In ten years, any man that loves me will die."

He studied her serious expression. "Now I really need to take notes," he decided.

"No. You need to go back to your archival work, to your dissertation, to your *family*, and forget about me."

"That's impossible, Violet." He shook his head. "I don't need these magical moments." He gestured to the ocean. "You were unforgettable from the moment I saw you. And this explains the fan. I wondered how you fixed it. Oh geez," he said excitedly.

Violet suddenly grabbed his arm and turned him slightly toward the house. "Take your shirt off."

"Anytime." He reached up for the back collar and pulled it off like all guys seemed to be able to do. If she wasn't so distracted by the hint of his tattoo she would have enjoyed watching but instead her stomach dropped once his tattoo was in full view.

Her fingers traced the overlapping keys on his shoulder. She just saw the tip of one from under his shirt but something about it screamed at her senses. "It's the papal keys," Phillip said softly, as if terrified that if he spoke too loudly he'd spook her, and he enjoyed having her fingers tracing his back. "My sister and I got them. Not identical," he said. He didn't know how to read her silence. "Don't tell me it's done something I can't see."

"I need to go."

"Violet." He grabbed her hand quickly. "Don't run from us."

"I don't want you to die," she admitted honestly. "Your sister, parents, friends—they don't want you to die."

"I don't want to either, but that's a problem for the future."

"You think if there was a solution we would have found it in three hundred years," Violet argued. "Yet time and again, every time a woman in my line falls in love and it's returned, he dies on the same day my ancestor's husband did."

"In the witch trial after Salem," he asked breathlessly.

She nodded and disappeared, his hand dropping down to his side.

As if expecting her, Abigail was reading a book in the study when Violet returned. "How could you?" Violet demanded.

"You found it."

"Him. You knew it was a man, not a damn lock."

"Symbolism, Vi."

"You can close up the house for Patience," Violet spat out before turning on her heel and leaving.

"That went well," Faith said from the entrance having overheard everything. "Need help?"

"No, go to your practice. I'll grab her stuff." Abigail sighed. "How long will she be mad at me you think?"

"Five years," Faith said morbidly.

Abigail popped into the house and found the room Violet was using. She materialized everything back to her room at home. Knowing the paints and paintings were more important to her sister than clothes, she planned on wrapping those in bubble wrap. She didn't need to give Violet another reason to be upset with her.

The sketchpad was open, and the first image was of a lock. Not the one in her dream, but this one screamed Violet. Abigail gently ripped the page out and materialized in Phillip's room just after he arrived home. He jumped, and she set it gently on the dresser.

"Do you know who I am?" she asked.

"One of Vi's sisters. The youngest, I think."

"Yup! I'm Abigail. I know you've talked about how we don't look alike. We're sisters but not related. We each have different parents but were raised together like a family. Because of the curse." Always the curse. "You should see this." She gestured to the paper. "It should mean something to you."

"Why are you here?"

"What has she told you?"

His gaze flicked upward with the back-and-forth volley of questions. Abigail knew he had to still be wrapping his head around what he saw and heard.

"That by loving her I'm dooming myself to die on a specific day."

"Vi is amazing. I love her. I also don't want her mad at me for the remaining five years of my life. She deserves to be loved. She doesn't agree because by loving her, you'll die. She's felt guilt over it since her own father passed. I'm guessing she didn't tell you about the whole curse."

"Whole curse?" His voice just slightly higher than normal.

"She dies too." He turned away and gripped the back of the chair at his old childhood desk. "Regardless of what happens between you. She is set to die on

June 2 of her thirty-fifth year. Just like her mother, and her mother, and all the women in her line. We all are cursed.”

“How have you not fixed things yet?”

“It’s hard when you are constantly dying,” Abigail deadpanned. “The D.E.M.O.N. daughters are cursed, and we haven’t figured out how to break it yet. The short, simple version is every generation we die at the same age, the same day, our original ancestors did in the witch trials.” Something was shifting, but she couldn’t articulate it yet, so she kept it to herself for now. “I wanted you to have that information while things percolated. Tata.” She smiled and disappeared in front of him.

He thought the hardest part would be accepting that Violet came from money—as soon as he saw the house in Swampscott he knew her family was well off while his was solidly working class.

Then she confirmed his absurd idea and *man*, watching her use her powers was a sight. He felt complete even though he didn’t know a piece of him had been missing. Until she tried to scare him off. Was he cautious? Usually. He intended to think about the fact he would die in ten years if he stayed but as he watched the ocean take back even their footprints, erasing any sign Violet had been on the beach, he knew it wasn’t a question—he had been absolutely sucker punched with this woman.

He looked at the drawing Abigail left behind and sucked in a breath. Centered was a rectangular padlock with leaves etching around the keyhole as if they were coming out from inside the lock and branched around the lock itself. He pulled his shirt off to look in the mirror. The etchings of his papal keys with the flow of branches and leaves looked identical.

Chapter Six

“I can’t explain the urgency, but she listens to you.” Abigail bit her lip as she ran one hand through her blond hair.

Patience could count the number of times Abigail was stressed on one hand, and while Violet had ignored all of them for a week now, this was the first time Abigail brought it up.

“Why? What’s going to happen?”

“I don’t know,” Abigail bit out, frustrated. “But something I haven’t felt before. And it scares me.”

“What do we need to get Violet to do?” Patience asked. If there was one thing she trusted, it was her sisters. If something scared Abigail, then it was going to be *hella* frightening.

“She has to admit her feelings. And soon. Something is coming,” Abigail warned. If she told Violet she would say the words but not mean them, and that would defeat the purpose. Even if she told her the thing was not coming for her but for Phillip.

"It's been over a week. I know in the grand scheme of things that's not long, but considering our time-bound lifespans, and whatever is coming, we need to do something now."

If any of them could get through to Violet it would be Patience. Closer in age, Violet saw herself as Patience's right hand in raising them.

Patience nodded as she grabbed her phone out of her back pocket. She was going to need the big guns for this one.

Violet saw her aunt come out the kitchen door to the patio. "Auntie," Violet said surprised. "What are you doing here?"

"I live on the other side of your lot. Do I need a reason to pop in and see my favorite niece?"

Violet smiled at the joke. Maxine viewed all the girls as her nieces. She stepped in to help Patience when their mothers all died. Violet, however, was her biological niece, and she was so thankful.

"You're my favorite aunt." Violet smiled.

"Patience called me. Join us," she called out to Patience lurking in the kitchen shadows. "I have news that you will want to know. But first, you, my darling. I hear you had such an adventure."

"Really, you called her over a boy?" Violet asked Patience, shocked.

"No, I called her over your dad."

At that, Violet just stared at Patience, then looked to see the knowing look her aunt gave her.

"We know you, sweet girl. You know the story of how your mother and my brother met. Have I ever told you who told me about the curse?"

"I assumed it was Daddy."

"No. He intended to, but your mother beat him to it. I won't tell you how she convinced me. That was quite a show. You can imagine. This white woman coming into my kitchen—mind you I was in an RV at the time—and saying she has powers and abilities and fell in love with my brother. As if that wasn't bat-shit crazy enough, once I believed her about the power, she told me about the curse."

"How did you not hate her?"

"Oh, I did. I told her to break it off. There was no way my brother was going to get involved with some crazy magic that would kill him in a decade. You know I couldn't stop either of them," she said matter-of-factly.

"'The heart wants what the heart wants,'" Violet repeated what her mother always said.

"I saw such guilt that day. Talk about an intense first meeting. I may have forbidden her from seeing my brother. Yes, I realize how ridiculous that sounds, but I was going to do what I could to protect him."

She looked at Violet with such maternal love it made Violet want to cry. Maxine's skin was darker than her own, like her father's had been, but they shared the same face shape and brown eyes. Having someone who was blood, who could share with her what her father's life and heritage was like as she grew up was priceless.

"You are so like your mother in this way. Do you know what your father told me?"

Violet shook her head. She'd never heard this story before. "I only ever knew the love at first sight story of their meeting. Dad meeting the sisters, the shower fiasco the first day..." Violet trailed off, laughing.

"You'll have to tell me that one again, but this is a night for a different story. A serious one because my brother was many things and that included serious when he needed to be. He came to me, infuriated as your mother tried to break it off with him."

"She did?" Violet asked shocked.

"I didn't realize then, but it was too late. Your father came to me and said he didn't want to make a choice, but he was going to be with the love of his life and their future daughter. I could either accept that or this was our goodbye."

"He couldn't mean that."

"The point, darling, is this: you have your mother's heart. You love fiercely. You have such a sense of fairness. You would sacrifice your feelings thinking they aren't worth the pain that will happen in the future. You are also your father's daughter. Serious. Fierce. Channel that now. Love can be worth it. Nothing in life is guaranteed. Your father knew what he was getting into, and once he made his choice, he was all in. He knew the risks and asked your mother to trust him. Follow his lead, trust your feelings, and trust *both* of you," Maxine implored. She took Violet's hand in hers. "I miss him. I know you do too. He had no regrets about his choice, Vi. Not even on that day."

Violet took the tissue Patience handed her as she ugly cried. "How do you know?"

"I saw him. He came by so I could make him breakfast like we had when we were kids. We had the chance to say goodbye. He was sad he would miss out on the rest, but knew you would turn into the compassionate, caring woman you are today."

Patience summoned a glass of water for Violet and wine for Maxine. Violet took a deep drink after blowing her nose. At least it was only her sister and aunt seeing her completely fall apart.

"It's only been a short time. How can he even know his feelings?" Violet asked.

"That's up to him. All you can do is decide your own," Patience said comfortingly.

"I..." She gulped another shot of water, closing her eyes. She never once saw her father sad—never once a sign of regret.

Nothing was guaranteed in life. Except her death. Set in stone. And Phillip's if she admitted it.

"I never pictured you as a coward, Vi." Patience stood. "I'm trying to be understanding. I know why you hesitate. Hell, how many nights did we discuss our futures? I would trade places with you in a heartbeat," she said pointedly.

"It's not that simple, *Pats*," Violet spat out, using the nickname Patience hated. "I love him, but there are complications!"

Patience smirked that big sister smirk of hers, and Violet realized what just happened. Maxine laughed, giving Patience a *good job* look.

"I love him," Violet repeated.

"You can be devastated," Patience said. "It's not easy, I know. Thank God." She sighed.

"What?" Violet asked.

"Something Abby said."

"I'm proud of you." Maxine smiled. "Now, my other news might distract you," she said somberly.

Suddenly, the kitchen door burst open with Abigail running frantically to them. "It's happening. Oh God," she said as Faith and Hannah followed her, sharing a concerned gaze.

Maxine managed to hide her reaction, but it was quite a sight: Abigail running out in yoga pants and top, her blond hair pulled back into a ponytail and her eyes were completely white with bands of gold twirling across her eyes as her powers flared with whatever vision she was seeing.

"What? What's wrong?" Patience jumped up.

"I didn't see what, but it wasn't human," Abigail said. "We have to hurry or we'll lose it. Phillip..."

"Phillip?" Violet demanded and disappeared before their eyes.

Violet appeared on a two-lane in the middle of the California desert with what used to be a car before her. It looked like something from a disaster film. Like it drove straight into something. The hood was completely smashed in, and the back half of the car pressed into the front half.

Except the road was completely empty.

"Hurry!" Hannah said suddenly beside her. "I smell gas."

"Phillip," Violet called out.

"Something is out there," Abigail said from where she, Faith, and Patience materialized in the middle of the road in front of the car.

"Why is he way out here?" Faith asked looking around at the desert they found themselves in.

"An aunt and uncle live closer to Palmdale. He must have gone to visit them," Patience said, telling them what she learned from her cyberstalking.

Hannah, her eyes completely white with gold sparking from heavy use, used her powers for strength and protection as she gripped the searing hot metal and pulled the door completely off the frame. As soon as Violet had an opening, she reached inside. Her fingers turned into claws to slash through the seatbelt.

"He's pinned in," she said.

"He'll be fine," Abigail called out to them.

"How the hell?" Hannah asked in disbelief.

"He knew his feelings." Abigail turned to them briefly as the leaking gas exploded, her hands stretching out and flinging around in a circle, directing the fire to form a circle around their party.

"One, two, three," Hannah said, and on three, she grabbed the frame where the door used to be hinged and pulled it back to unpin Phillip.

Violet wasn't sure how he was alive, but he was as she pulled him out.

She cradled him close a safe distance between the car and the fire and took a good look around for the first time. "What the hell happened?"

There was nothing. Absolutely nothing. Not even skid marks. So whatever happened occurred while Phillip was driving at full speed.

"It's still here," Abigail said, staring out into the night.

Faith glared into the night. She raised a hand to part the fire in front of them, pillars shooting flame several yards high. "Show yourself," she called out. "Or are you a coward who attacks unsuspecting humans only?"

"Do you have to antagonize it?" Patience muttered, thinking she'd feel better if she knew *what* they were up against.

Suddenly, Abigail's arms stretched out, and she waved her right hand like a conductor for a moment. The fire followed her directions, scissoring across the desert landscape and chasing whatever it was they couldn't see. Where the fire trailed after it, Joshua trees erupted in flames like Roman candles.

Faith looked up and waved her hand at the sky. The clouds covering the moon moved to give them even more light. Despite the extra light, they couldn't see anything.

"Whatever it was, it's gone," Abigail said. The fire extinguished as soon as she said that.

"What the hell was it?" Patience asked.

"Should we go to the hospital?" Violet asked from where she was cradling Phillip.

Abigail came to kneel before them, her white eyes meeting Violet's matching white eyes. "He knew his feelings. Now you know yours. Just in time. The curse will keep him alive," Abigail promised.

"We should get out of here," Hannah said.

"I'll clean things up here," Patience said, looking around. Faith and Hannah volunteered to stay behind with her—strength in numbers after all.

Violet materialized with Phillip in their living room.

Their aunt heard them and came in. "Holy hell, what happened?"

"He was in the car," Violet tried to explain but started shaking.

Abigail pulled a blanket from the back of the couch to wrap around her as their aunt came to look at Phillip.

"I don't know how he is alive, but I would guess in five minutes, he'll be even better than he is now," Maxine finally said, recognizing the curse kicking in and keeping the man alive.

"Should we bring him to the ER? Abduct a doctor?" Violet asked, and Abigail burst out laughing. "*What?*"

"You went from not acknowledging your feelings to abducting a doctor in twenty minutes," she said, and even Violet had to smile.

"What happened?" Maxine repeated as the other girls arrived.

"To be honest, we're not sure," Faith said, exhausted.

They had reversed any damage the fire had done, moved the car into the desert off the road, and set it on fire. Hopefully, whoever found it would think it was kids mucking around.

"It wasn't human," Abigail said from where she was crouched next to Violet and Phillip. She ran her hands over Phillip's abdomen slowly, chains of gold rippling in her all-white eyes as she used an immense amount of power to aid in his healing.

Just because the curse wouldn't let him die didn't mean he had to suffer.

Violet had cleared the head trauma and nearly dropped his head when his eyes opened.

"Vi? Mmm, this is a nice dream." He moaned in pain.

"Not a dream, lover boy," Faith drawled.

His eyes shot open to see he was in a living room he didn't recognize. "Not how I planned on meeting your sisters," he said slowly. "Uh, hi. And, uh, question, what happened?"

"What do you remember?" Patience asked.

"Driving. Then nothing. It… I don't know what. I was driving, and suddenly, it was like my car hit a brick wall. Everything started to compact, compress…" He winced, reliving the memory of pain like he had never known before blackness.

"It wasn't human. That's all we know."

"That's unexpected."

"I like him." Faith grinned causing several snickers.

"What hurts the worst?" Violet asked.

"I can't feel my legs. The stomach pain is fading," he said.

"Almost done with that," Abigail said cheerfully from where she was straddling his thighs with her hands over his abdomen.

"Second question," he said slowly. "My brain isn't firing on all cylinders." But it was quickly catching up. "How am I alive?"

"We'll let Violet answer that one," Patience said.

"I think he is good enough to rest in a proper bed," Maxine said. "You won't be able to walk yet. Your internal injuries were more important for Abby to deal with than your legs."

"I'm just thrilled to be here," Phillip said truthfully. "Assuming I'm not in fact dead."

"Sleep," Violet said and kissed his forehead, putting him into a deep, healing sleep.

"Thank you," Violet told Abigail before she materialized them to her room so he could sleep in her bed.

"You never said your news, Auntie," Violet said as she brought them both out some tea. She was too frightened to sleep, worried they missed something while healing Phillip. She also knew between Abigail and the curse he would be fine and didn't need her fretting and watching him sleep. Then she remembered her Aunt had something to share so Violet decided to distract herself and sought out her aunt.

"I thought it best to warn Patience. Now I'm not so sure." Maxine exhaled a long sigh, tension Violet didn't notice earlier coiled up in her aunt's shoulders and face. "It's about your cousin."

"Rose?" Violet asked, perplexed. Violent never saw her aunt indecisive.

"No, not my daughter. My son."

Violet looked at her surprised. He wasn't exactly taboo, but even Maxine didn't talk about him in their house out of respect for Patience.

"He's okay." She would sense if something happened to her cousins.

"Yes. He's coming home."

"Holy shit."

Chapter Seven

Phillip woke, and for a single moment before opening his eyes, it was a normal day—drink coffee, make lesson plans for that new job (*holy crap what am I doing?*), and grab dinner with his aunt and uncle.

Then he remembered that was yesterday, and his eyes snapped open. The room was definitely not his. First, there was real furniture, not his graduate-student-cheap furniture. The walls were a soft green with art—lots of art.

And the artist was sleeping next to him, her black hair splayed out behind her head.

He gently stroked her hair, and her eyes snapped open. "How are you feeling?" Worried chocolate-colored eyes raked over his body.

"Considering I should be dead, amazing," he reminded her.

"How much do you remember?"

How was her hair so soft? Maybe his senses were in hyper overdrive after his near-death experience. His brain was certainly kicking into high gear as he remembered last night.

"I went to go to my aunt and uncle's," he said. "Shit, they're probably worried."

"I texted them from your phone, pretending to be you. I said you had a car accident. You were fine but couldn't make it up."

"They bought that?"

Violet grinned and raised her hand, his phone flying from the side table to land in her palm. She managed to bypass the lock screen with the tap of her finger and brought up his text. "I didn't go snooping, but I didn't want them to come looking for you or worry. We weren't sure if they would be attacked if they showed up. Probably not, but we didn't want to risk it." Violet handed him his phone.

He saw the text to his aunt, which included a photo of him in front of a smashed up car on the side of the highway. "That was definitely not me," Phillip stated the obvious. Mostly because there was so much he didn't know, so he stuck to what he did—he was too busy not dying to be taking photos.

Violet grinned impishly as he pushed himself up to lean against the headboard. "Look in your photo gallery."

He opened it up and nearly dropped his phone on the bed. The first several photos were of him—there were *three* of him—taking selfies in front of his wrecked car. "Am I seeing triple?"

Violet laughed as she sat up so they were eye level with each other. "They had a little fun. Any pain anywhere?" She bit her lip as she studied him.

"No. How?"

"What do you remember?"

"I was driving. It was late, dark. You know 18," he said, naming the highway that went up into the High Desert part of Southern California. "It was a ghost town. Suddenly, it was like I was one of those test crash dummies. The car was slamming into something. It was slow motion. I couldn't see anything, and I should have—I was the only one on the highway," he tried to rationalize. "I could see my car folding in on itself, feel it."

"You're okay," she promised, one hand coming up to trace along his jaw. "My sisters and I got you out. We don't know what it was, though. It got away before we could get it."

"What was it? Wait, you just said you don't know," he realized, running his hand through his hair. "It's not every day I don't die from a fatal accident. So, next question: how am I not dead? Not questioning your powers, but I had to be dead when you got there. Can you raise the dead?"

"No, we can't. You were unconscious. We got you out before your car exploded. Something was there, but we don't know what. I brought you back here. My aunt is a nurse."

"She would have to have power like you."

She laughed, and he swore the sound made his heart flutter.

"She's human, completely, but a total bad ass in her own right," Violet declared proudly. "It was mostly Abigail, working on the things my aunt said were the most important to fix first. Your legs were last. I took a pass at them last night. Do you think you can stand?"

"I would normally prefer to stay in bed with you, but my curiosity is piqued," he admitted, catching the barest glimmer of a blush as he turned to swing his legs over the side of the bed. He found himself hesitating as flashbacks of his car pressing into his legs and nearly severing them came to mind.

Suddenly, Violet's worried face came into his vision. She had come around the bed to help if need be.

He didn't feel any pain—in fact, he felt normal. How was that possible? He wasn't dumb enough to refuse her offered hand, though. The last time he was awake and alert to feel her touch was weeks ago when he confronted her about her powers.

He stood on his own two bare feet, looking down at them. "I don't know how, but I feel better than I did before the thing." *Accident* wasn't the right word, he didn't know what to call it.

"Good enough to walk downstairs?" she asked.

"Pretty sure I could jump down a flight of stairs, which is mind boggling." He looked around the room and couldn't tell what time of day it was with curtains drawn over the windows.

"The room suits you." He saw the time on her wall clock. "How is it only going on nine a.m.?" he asked, surprised. "Wait, how many days?"

"It's the following morning," she said. "Let's get some food into you. I'm starving." With a flick of her wrist, the curtains parted to let in the sunlight.

He stood by his earlier statement—the room *felt* like Violet: artistic, subtle, powerful, feminine.

"I told everyone not to overwhelm you. I was only promised breakfast," she warned him.

"I don't know where I am or what to expect," he said.

Her playful grin tugged at his heart. "The family home in the Hollywood Hills."

"Okay, that's half of it."

She laughed as she opened the door, and they exited into a hallway. Violet's room was at the end of the hallway with a closed door opposite. Light from the window above them at the end of the corridor flooded the hallway. All he could tell was there were several doors on either side of a long hall with a staircase heading down.

He felt the wealth. He didn't know how to explain any of the architectural things he saw or know how many of the doors he could see led to bedrooms, but he knew there was more than he could see. He was pretty sure this floor alone was twice the size of his parents' house back in Boston.

They reached the landing, and it overlooked the entranceway. He worried he would look ridiculous trying to look around like a kid in a toy store for the first time.

"What do you like for breakfast?" Violet's voice brought him out of his thoughts.

"Coffee."

Violet rolled her eyes. "And for food?"

"I'm content with whatever." He wasn't picky and wasn't rushing out the door to class, grabbing whatever was handy.

Violet took his hand again, and that grounded him. Especially when they turned and he saw what was clearly a music room. The grand piano ensured anyone walking by would take notice.

Violet led him to the kitchen and deposited him into the booth in the corner. It gave him the chance to look around while she made him his coffee, exactly how he liked it, before pulling things from the refrigerator and cupboards.

The island easily doubled for casual dining, and he wondered if this was where they ate when they ate together. How often was that?

"You said family home," he repeated as the coffee chased away the last of the cobwebs. "Who all lives here?"

Violet grabbed a plate and some paper towels to drain the bacon she had going, wondering how it was possible that Phillip was *here*, alive and drinking coffee in their kitchen. The thought of the alternative was too much to think about—not that she couldn't stop thinking about it last night as she watched his breathing, terrified he would stop breathing if she didn't watch him like a hawk.

"We all do, mostly. Faith does have a dorm she stays at during the week usually. She rooms with her partner—a volleyball partner," Violet quickly added. "Although, with it being summer, she is deep into the season so not around as much. Hannah gave the dorms a try her first year and decided she didn't like it, so she commutes."

"That leaves Abigail and Patience."

"Patience runs the home." Violet smiled as she tossed some of the sourdough in to toast. "Avocado or butter?" she asked. "For the toast."

"Butter."

"Patience keeps everything going," Violet continued. "She's working—her office is past the music room down the hall. Abigail, well, she tends to do what she wants."

"That seems to fit."

Violet grabbed the two plates—one for each of them—and carried them over. "What do you mean?"

"I met her, once," he admitted.

She sat down with extra *plump* on the bench next to him. "Wait, what? When? Why?" Violet sighed as she picked up a slice of bacon. "I'm not surprised."

Phillip laughed into his coffee, watching her run the gamut of emotions. "Why not?"

"She beats to her own drum."

"After I confronted you, I took the train back down to Boston. Every minute made me madder thinking about how you simply disappeared. I was definitely filled with righteous anger when I reached my parents' house and stormed into my old bedroom where I was staying, and I turn around—and there she is."

"Why?" Violet wondered, grabbing her own coffee. "That would have been after I told her to go pack up the house in Swampscott."

"She told me a bit more about the curse—things you should have told me." He frowned at her. "Then she left me a drawing, one of your drawings, before disappearing."

"That sounds like her," Violet said. "Which drawing?"

"One of a lock. It matched the design of my tattoo."

The same tattoo she saw on the beach when he confronted her, which had freaked her out. A woman who had parted the sea at their feet without breaking a sweat but panicked seeing his tattoo of the papal keys.

Keys that were surrounded by bramble and leaves, matching the design of the lock she had drawn.

"I am beginning to realize just how amazing it was that my dad stayed for all this. I don't even know where to start explaining things. My aunt—my dad's sister—and my cousin live on the property, too, in the chauffeur's cottage."

"Chauffeur? I thought your aunt was a nurse?"

Violet grinned. "She is. My cousin is starting college, and we kind of bullied her into living on campus. But she's here more often than not. When the grandmothers bought the property back in the forties, they bought a couple of lots—privacy," she explained. "Hard to dance naked in the moonlight with nosey neighbors." She laughed when Phillip choked on his toast. "We only do that on special occasions. Don't worry. There's a few buildings on the property since we never put in the pool as the architects originally planned."

"Why look at your eventual death on a daily basis? I understand that."

"Hannah and I. We're both destined to drown," Violet said as she grabbed both their plates. "I'm not afraid, not really, but I appreciate not looking at a giant source of my impending death on the daily. Faith... You'll meet her. She is the type to build it just to give it the middle finger every morning." Faith didn't drown, and bravado aside, wouldn't do something that tormented Violet's sanity.

Phillip smiled as he studied her, which made her heartbeat triple. "How are you not running for the hills?"

"Couldn't go far. We're already in the hills."

"Haha." Violet rolled her eyes. "What I've told you already is enough for someone to commit me to the insane asylum."

He studied her, and she wanted to curl up next to him. How did he make her want to turn into a cat and cuddle on his lap, purring in contentment?

"Before I confronted you, I had to have a come-to-Jesus moment with myself. Was I really going up to this woman I was falling fast for to declare you were a witch? I'm from Boston, for crying out loud. I had to mentally wrap myself around the idea that if I believed it was a possibility, I would have to accept it if it was true. I don't know if that makes sense. Everything since then—you parting the ocean, your sister materializing in my bedroom and then disappearing, dying but not dying—I don't know what else could explain all that. Unless I am dead, and this is all some weird afterlife. But I don't know what the point of it would be, so I'm going with this is still the real deal."

"Are you sure you're not a philosophy major?" Violet teased, making him blushed. *Could he be any more adorable?*

"I do need to work on the new job," he admitted quickly. "The school year starts at the end of the month."

"Of course," Violet said, wondering if there was a shift in the air suddenly or if she was making that up in her head. "I can take you to your apartment, or you can use my car," she volunteered.

"Really?"

"I can get where I need to go without it," Violet pointed out. She brought her hand up, closed then opened her palm, and car keys appeared. "Are you up for driving?"

"In the city, sure. I'll be honest. I might not be up for the drive up to my aunt and uncle any time soon."

She gripped his hand, taking it in both of hers. "Will you come back tonight? I would like you to meet everyone. And I'm sure you'll have more questions."

"Since I'm part of this, I'm assuming?"

She nodded.

"I'll be back. Let me know if there's a certain time you need me."

She walked him to the garage—well, one of them—where all their daily cars were. She felt a little tingle of fear at him leaving so soon after the attack, so she slipped her hand into his.

As if sensing it—perhaps wishful thinking on her part—he brought her hand up to his to kiss. His body turned toward her, and his other hand came up to gently wrap around her waist as he moved in to kiss her properly.

"I'll be back tonight," he assured her before turning to the car.

She rubbed her finger under her lips where they kissed as she watched him drive off.

"You okay?" Patience said from behind her, interrupting her thoughts.

Violet shook her head, and Patience wrapped her in a hug. "I feel like he's running away, which would be the sane thing to do. He nearly died, and yet it's breaking my heart."

"He didn't have to stay for breakfast if he was just going to run away," Patience said after a moment. "I think he needs to process. Which, let's face it, makes sense.

He nearly died, he's in love with a kick-ass witch, and he found out he's cursed now. It's a lot to take in."

Violet leaned her head against her sister's. "I hope so. If I was a minute later…" she trailed off. The thought was too big, too scary to complete.

"You weren't. Abby wouldn't let you." Patience laughed. "And if he doesn't adjust quickly, I'll kick his ass for you."

Violet laughed and decided everything was right in the world again. Then she remembered in all the chaos, no one told Patience that Aunt Maxine's son was finally coming home.

"I'm going to see if Rose is here. Thanks." Violet hugged Patience before heading to her aunt's house. Maybe he wasn't actually coming back to SoCal, just to the states. Maybe he would be stationed somewhere like Virginia.

Violet feared Patience wasn't that lucky.

<h1 style="text-align:center">Chapter Eight</h1>

Traffic in California being what it was, Phillip had plenty of time to berate himself on the drive to his apartment.

If you tried, you could have run a little faster. Violet had to have noticed. She wasn't dumb, deaf, or blind.

His sister sitting on his couch when he walked in was the last thing he needed.

"So you're alive after all," she drawled. "'My car is totaled, but I'm fine. Call you tomorrow,'" Colleen mimicked, repeating the text Violet had sent. "Take your time. It's not like I knew where to find you, and you weren't answering your phone."

"Can you hold off, C?" He stormed into the kitchen and pulled out the water pitcher from the fridge then a glass from the cupboard opposite.

She followed after him but never crossed the threshold. Considering how small the apartment was, he didn't blame her. "Well, you look physically fine. You really called this woman you've been dating for, what, like a month instead of me?!"

"That's what you're pissed about?"

"Why are you worked up?" she demanded. "I'm the one who spent the night worried sick."

"I told you I was fine."

"Nothing about that text was fine."

"If it makes you feel better, I made a fool of myself and haven't even met the rest of her family, which was supposed to be the most awkward part of everything. Damn it!"

That caught her attention. "Start at the beginning. You were going up to Palmdale and shitty driver..."

"Something like that," Phillip drawled, leaning against the now-closed refrigerator door after he replaced the water pitcher. How to explain what was unexplainable to his sister? He was shocked when he believed everything about the curse before the crash because it didn't seem real—witches? Powers? Curses? *Who was he*? He enjoyed rummaging around documents older than the country with gloves and a pencil to find evidence of historical events.

And how could he tell his sister everything only to make her worry for the next decade before he died?

"I was talking to Violet on the phone when it happened, so she knew. Her place was closer, so I crashed there. Once the adrenaline was gone, I passed out," he lied. *You're protecting her*, he told himself.

"Then I wake up and realize what I knew but never had to face before—she's rich. Like, *rich*, C."

"I mean, you said Hollywood Hills. Like, way up in the hills, so I kind of thought, '*Go, Phillip*,'" she teased. She leaned against the counter to study him. "What's wrong?"

"She's leading me to the kitchen and offering to make breakfast, and I'm like 'holy shit that music room is larger than this apartment,' and realizing our parent's home would fit on one level with room left over."

"And?"

"And?" he asked, perplexed. "I practically tripped over my own feet running out of there when she lent me her car because they have a collection."

"The Ford is hers?" Colleen jerked her thumb towards the street. "I was wondering. She has a collection of Fords? Like different colors?"

"Why are you teasing me in my time of need?" he huffed, eyes wide as he looked puzzled.

Colleen laughed and hugged him, holding on longer than needed. "First, you're okay. I'm still pissed as hell for scaring me. Second, why does the money scare you?"

"I didn't know it would. I don't know why."

"Well, figure it out with that big brain of yours. She doesn't seem to care you are slumming it in the Valley." She gestured around his shoe-box sized kitchen behind him as if to prove her point. "She does know you are slumming it, right? At least you don't have any ruffians as roommates anymore."

"Hey, I know you happened to like one of them."

"Now he has jokes. I kind of get it," she said slowly with a nod. "I haven't dated anyone with money, but I'm around them because of work. It is a different lifestyle, different rules."

"But?" He could practically hear what she left unsaid and hoped for pearls of wisdom.

"But you're not an idiot, and you're not shallow. You wouldn't fall for someone who was an idiot, nor would you be with someone just because they have money. That tells me she must be a great person, and I demand I meet her. This weekend, Aunt Siobhan texted that they are hosting a neighborhood thing before school starts for their kids next week. Bring Violet."

"I'll ask."

"Good. Now a music room? What else did you see when you weren't tripping over your feet?"

"Har, har. I don't know. I don't know how to talk about architecture. Massive house, with extensive grounds. The Ford is an all-electric Mustang and was parked between an all-electric Porsche and all-electric BMW. Her aunt lives on the property in what she called the *chauffeur house*."

"Hot damn, you weren't lying about having money," Collen said surprised. She studied her brother. "You were going to prep for the new job today, but you're going to be learning architecture now, aren't you? You'll have a degree in it by the time you're done."

"Again, my time of need." He pretended to pout with a hand over his heart. He knew she loved him even if they were polar opposites. She saw lines and color and texture, while he wanted to know the how and why.

"What can I say? I'm thinking this Violet will be good for you."

Phillip pulled in right before six, like his text said. She knew he would, but Violet still wouldn't blame him if he ran for the beach instead of the hills in this case.

"Hey."

"Hi." His smile reached his eyes, and that soothed some of her nerves. Amazing how after a short time she came to be looking forward to seeing his smiles.

She leaned against his chest when he wrapped his arms around her, and she took a moment to breathe him in. "No pain?"

"It could almost have been a dream, the way everything is back to normal. A scar from my childhood even healed up," he said in shock. "Thankfully, the tattoo is untouched."

Violet grinned as she took his hand. "I'm sorry. I feel like I'm throwing you into the deep end."

"Consider me returning the favor this weekend, then. My aunt and uncle are doing a neighborhood barbeque before school starts for the kids next week. They want me to bring you so you can meet them and my sister."

"Want me to drive?"

"Hell yes."

His quick response made her laugh. He held the back door open for her to enter first. She felt him nervously stiffen behind her when he entered and saw everyone.

"Guys, this is Phillip. Phillip, this is my family," Violet said.

"For crying out loud, we've seen him half-naked. Come on in."

Laughing, Violet took Phillip's hand. The tension was gone. "That was Faith," Violet rolled her eyes. They would start at that end of the table, then. "The second youngest. You met Abigail, apparently." Violet glared at her youngest sister.

"Wait, when?"

"That's Hannah, the middle sister." Violet nodded to the redhead who asked the question. She nodded to Patience who stood. "Patience."

Patience offered her hand to Phillip before going to answer the front door. She returned a moment later with several boxes of pizza.

"My cousin Rosemary."

"Family and friends call me Rose." Rosemary waved from her seat at the table.

"My aunt, my father's sister, Maxine," Violet introduced completely the introductions.

Maxine stood and took one of his hands in both of hers. Having known her all her life, Violet knew her aunt was sizing him up, and she was one of the two people she was dying to know what they thought. "Welcome to the family, Phillip."

Violet beamed, and took a quick look at Patience. They were closest in age, and were the closest growing up. As if sensing her thought Patience looked up from the pizza boxes and gave her an affectionate smile. Just like that, Violet looked around and knew they all accepted him. Relief flooded her, and she realized she had been nervous to be the first to bring in a guy to the family.

"Thank you."

"We'll grill him later, Vi. Come on, I am starving," Faith said as she waved at a cupboard, and a cabinet door burst open with plates flying out and into a pile near the stack of pizza boxes.

"I thought we agreed to keep it low-key tonight?" Hannah barked at her.

"I refuse to die of hunger in my own house." Faith shrugged. "Besides, we saved his life from some sort of supernatural attack, and you think *dishes* are going to make him run for the hills?"

"If anyone has the right to be annoyed, I'm pointing out it was not my turn to take care of dinner," Patience threw into the mix. "You don't hear me complaining." Patience turned to Phillip. "We weren't sure what you liked, so we got the basics. Nothing with sardines or pineapple, though."

"*Ew* to both," Phillip promised.

"See! I told you he'd fit in," Abigail proclaimed. "Violet stocked the fridge with some of your drinks," she added and pointed to what looked like a cupboard door.

When he pulled it open, it revealed a fridge.

"Yes, we have two." Violet laughed when he did a double take to look at the French door fridge across the kitchen. "There's a minimum of five people living here at all times. At one point, with our mothers, many more. We eat a lot."

"Thanks for thinking of me," he said as he grabbed the soda.

Everyone piled food onto plates. Breadsticks were divided onto two platters and set on the table.

And it blew her mind that Phillip was here with them. It had been girls' only, what Patience called *the Sisterhood*, for so long.

"I can't believe you aren't peppering us with questions," Patience admitted.

"He's keeping a list." Abigail grinned.

"Do you know what they are?" he wondered.

"Yes. No. Sometimes. Only on Fridays. Some of us."

"And now for the questions." Hannah grinned at Phillip.

"'*Do you know what they are?*' was the first, and that's a yes," Abigail pointed out.

"Can you read minds? Oh." Phillip's eyes widened. "No. That's a relief, probably. Do you do these family meals all the time, and do you all live here? I think you gave more answers than I had questions."

"Did I?" Abigail asked innocently.

"There's a dinner schedule. I'll show you," Violet promised, wondering what Abigail was up to.

"Anyone is welcome any time," Patience said. "We don't always sit down to eat together anymore—hence, sometimes—but we do when we can and our schedules line up. Although pizza is usually on Fridays."

"Oh," Phillip said, straightening in his seat for a moment, his eyes widening.

"He just realized something." Abigail raised an eyebrow.

"That having a psychic in the house is going to take some getting used to."

Abigail's grin could have been in the dictionary under mischief.

Later, Violet asked him to stay the night. They were sitting outside under the tree her father had planted for her when she was born.

"This isn't the chauffeur's house," Phillip noted.

"No. The Bungalow. My parents lived here, with me, for most of my life before they died. I always had a room in the house," she explained quickly. "But my dad was the only man here in our mothers' generation, so they made the cottage their place."

"Wait, what do you mean the only man?"

"I don't know how we have managed to avoid talking about the curse until now," Violet sighed. "I kept waiting for you to ask questions all day, then during dinner."

"I have them. Don't worry. Lots of them," he promised. "Partly, I don't know where to start. But also, meeting your family was a big deal on its own, Vi. We may be stuck together, all of us, because of the curse, but that doesn't mean I don't care if they like me or not."

Violet took his hand, absently tracing her fingers over his palm. "Everything goes back to the first generation, the original *D.E.M.O.N.* daughters. What happened to their line reciprocates down to us. The *E*, *M*, and *N* lines have potential. They were happily married to good men. Men who died for them. Every generation, there's the potential for us three to experience the same. My mother met and fell for my father, bringing him into this curse."

"Where he died the same day as your mother."

She nodded. "Because the men died in an attempt to protect our ancestors, they keep dying. Hannah's mother didn't have anyone. I don't know all the backstory. I was young when she died, but she never showed any interest in anyone that I know of. Abigail's mother did. I don't remember him. I was too young when they died."

"You drown."

It was a statement, but Violet nodded. "Every generation. Hannah and I both do."

"Will I?"

"No." Violet shook her head and took a deep breath. "Same deaths as the original daughters. Hannah and I drown. You are shot."

The pregnant silence nearly made her pull at her hair. "What are you thinking?"

"So far, it seems like the easiest death."

"The man in the Milan line is crushed to death. No one is sure exactly about the Neapolis line. No one witnessed it, so we don't have a record. What we know is he always dies two weeks before the baby is born, regardless if he's the father or not."

"What?"

"Being the biological father isn't what determines it. It's the connection between the two. A couple generations ago, the Neapolis became pregnant by someone else—knowingly. She and her husband knew. She was trying to save his life. It didn't work. They both still died as the curse directs."

He used one hand to cup her face, his eyes darkened with emotion. "For the record, I'm not going through all this and you sleep with someone else."

Violet grinned. "Noted."

"What about the Dubrovnik and Orleans line? Patience and Faith?"

"Both were betrayed by the father of their child. Neither ever have a healthy relationship, and it always ends with the father, or the man they want to be the father, betraying them somehow."

She leaned against him as they laid back and looked up at the stars. "You're taking this in a lot better than I imagined."

"I have a decade to process," he said. "Deciding what order to ask questions. The historian in me *needs* to find more resources on this, but I can hear my sister telling me that asking for primary documents is not sexy and I'd ruin the moment."

Violet snorted, slapping a hand over her mouth. She wasn't supposed to do anything embarrassing in front of him, at least not for the foreseeable future. "I'd be more upset if you didn't," she promised. "You are this Clark Kent-inspired nerd."

"I don't know if that's an insult or not."

"Definitely not." Violet turned towards him to kiss him. When they broke apart, she sat up on her knees and leaned back. "Come on, I have something to show you."

"Besides your massive house?"

She looked at him in confusion. "I should have given you a tour. I'm sorry. This morning was crazy. There's nothing off limits, nothing like that. No 'don't go into the locked room' or anything like that."

"I didn't mean that." He sighed and sat up. "I'm between roommates right now with an apartment in the Valley. My parents own their own home, but for things like college, we had to take out loans or find other ways to pay."

"Okay," Violet trailed off, wondering where this was going.

"My parents' house would fit in one floor of your house with room to spare."

"So?" She took his hand, entertaining their fingers. "The money—thanks mostly to Faith's great-grandmother and good investments since then—gave me that breathing room so I could do what I wanted. I know I'm blessed with that. But it doesn't change that I didn't go to college, never took a college class. I never cared. But then I met this guy working on his PhD, and suddenly, I found myself questioning my decisions. I never even went to art school. I simply dove in."

He brought her hand up to kiss her palm, his face softened. "He's a lucky guy—this guy working on his PhD."

"Some might question that, seeing as how he's now cursed."

"Hmm. About that..." Phillip helped Violet to her feet. "Do you have any original documents?"

Violet laughed but led him through the house and up to the attic on the third floor. She threw open the door and flipped the light switch. "It's far from 'Gandalf reading in Minas Tirith' and absolutely modern. I doubt there's a cobweb in sight. I'm pretty sure Patience has banished all bugs from the house."

"Well, those hopes are dashed." Phillip smiled and couldn't resist running one hand through her hair, running loosely down her back. "It comes with a girl who makes *Lord of the Rings* references, so I'll take it."

"Book *and* movie, mind you." Violet smiled. She gestured widely to the large room.

In the daylight, the windows had to let in massive amounts of sunlight. He could probably work without the overhead lights.

"I'm pretty sure it is only stuff since our great-grandmothers had the property developed. I haven't been up here in ages, to be honest."

"They were the first in California?"

Violet nodded. "Not born, but came together. Faith's great-grandmother... I think it was her great-grandmother? Yes. Chastity O. as she was called. She caught the eyes of several producers, made a few silent movies, but she was one of the lucky ones, able to transition to the talkies. She was cute, could sing and dance, and her natural voice was thought to be conventional yet beautiful. She made two films before dying tragically at the young age of twenty-five in a fiery car accident. Her body was unable to be recovered."

"So Faith's line dies at twenty-five?"

"By fire." Violet nodded. "She had a torrid affair with another actor that led to Faith's grandmother. Chastity bought this property, but I don't think she ever saw the home completed."

"So many questions." Phillip sighed and lifted the lid to a box. Inside were photo albums, old from what he could tell, so definitely not Violet or her sisters.

"Grandmas." Violet smiled, coming over to look. "So this must be that generation over here. I feel like Patience would have organized by generation."

"Not by family?"

"No?" Violet said, her voice inflecting like it never occurred to her. "Were you wanting to start with a specific person? Family? Time period?"

"I'm mostly curious what you have here that is the oldest, and from whom. And by curious, I mean *absolutely* dying. Like *holy shit* you have a signed polaroid with Elvis," he said as he gently lifted one of the photo albums and it fluttered out. "How is that not better preserved?"

She mimed fanning him. "I'm beginning to think you aren't up for the deep dive that is spelunking through our family's junk. Not so soon after the attack, anyway."

"Your family's 'junk'—never use that word around a historian—is about five cursed family lines," he pointed out.

"Here." She took the polaroid, and it was suddenly encased in what looked like glass. "Happy?" She smiled.

"This may give me heart palpitations, but let's see if we can find your great-grandmothers. The further back we go, the more information we have."

"You are looking for something."

"Information," he said easily, looking at her bewildered. "Information is a weapon, and we need to find three hundred years' worth of it."

Chapter Nine

Deciding the best way to get over being intimidated was to throw himself into the deep end—metaphorically speaking—Phillip decided to look around and explore the house in the morning. He tried not to think about it last night when they walked through, as if avoiding looking inside dark rooms would hide how large the house was. Sometime last night he decided the house would always be intimidating until he decided it wasn't. If he didn't want Violet to hold his working-class background against him, he couldn't hold her family's wealth against her.

He was also floored at Violet's implication that *she* was in any way intimidated by *him*. He agreed he was a nerd and getting his doctorate screamed nerd, but he never imagined it would be even remotely intimidating.

Starting downstairs, he went with what he already knew and went to the music room first after grabbing some coffee. The music room doubled as a library, he discovered. The piano was a Steinway, and while he had no musical talent, he knew the name.

"Sorry!"

He spun around to see Hannah starting to retreat. "No, wait. I think I'm intruding on your time," he said. "I didn't think anyone else was up, so I thought I'd surreptitiously explore." He blushed.

"It's nearly eight a.m. Patience has been up for over an hour, I'd guess." Hannah smiled, and he could see caution on her face.

Violet had described her as fairy-like, and he had no idea what she had meant till now. He was a bit overwhelmed at dinner last night, and the truth was the sisters together exuded an intensity he had never seen before. *That* was intimidating. On her own now, though, Phillip realized what Violet meant. Hannah had ethereal red hair he was sure was being spotlighted by an invisible lamp. Tall and willowy, she put him in mind of one of Tolkien's elves.

"I'm guessing you were going to play, I'll get out of your way."

"Don't let me stop you from exploring." Hannah smiled easily. "I can play anytime and in several places. It was more I'm not used to seeing someone new around."

"I hope I can hear you play sometime. Violet has told me about your talent."

Hannah gave him a small smile as she tilted her head to look upward toward Violet's room. "You two were up late. I'm surprised you're up."

"Finally found your great-grandmother's section of the attic. But I've been meaning to look up some of your work for a while, ever since she told me. I told my sister, and she found the clips of you body doubling in a few different movies, none of which she worked on."

"Wait, when did she tell you?"

"Um, a few weeks ago?" Phillip tried to think as he took a sip of his coffee. "I can't remember exactly. It was one of our day trips."

Hannah's smile lit up her whole face. "That's all right. I have a meeting later with a friend, so I thought I'd get in a little time this morning. Feel free to stay if you like." She smiled as she walked over to the piano, running a scale to check it was still in tune from yesterday.

Violet found him looking through a few of the books while Hannah played. More accurately, he was pretending to look through books but never turning a page while her sister played.

"Is there a reason you are stuck on page seventeen?" Violet whispered.

He gently placed the book back and nodded toward the kitchen. He waited till they were inside and he poured himself a refill of his coffee. "I knew your sister had to be good, but *man*. I started to look at the books because I thought I might disturb her with my presence. Turns out, I don't think she'd notice if I came or went."

Violet beamed, always proud of her sister. "She did. I'm sure. She simply doesn't care. Unless you hated the music, then she would probably levitate objects to send directly at your head while playing Brahms—from memory."

He shook his head, amused. "I can check off meeting my first musical prodigy to my bucket list. A bucket list I didn't know I had at the beginning of summer, but one I'm enjoying." He leaned back against the counter and watched Violet doctor her coffee. "She seemed surprised when we were talking earlier that I knew about her."

"Hannah is many things, including the middle child," Violet said before taking a long drink of her coffee. "And she is *very* much the middle child. I sometimes..." she trailed off as she gathered her thoughts. "Patience and I are only a year apart. Fath and Abigail less than. Hannah's only a year older than Faith, but Faith and Abby have always been inseparable. Their lifespans are both the shortest, with Faith only a year longer than Abby's. Hannah had someone, a boy who was with us for a few years, but he went on to live with his aunt and uncle, and I sometimes worry she's been lonely ever since."

He wrapped his arm around her waist as she sipped her coffee. "Maybe I need to start getting you prepared for the neighborhood bash at my aunt's and uncle's, with my very mundane, very normal, suburban family. I have to warn you, it will be quite bland compared to life here." He gave her a boyish grin making her laugh.

She leaned into him before taking a sip of her coffee. "I can handle normal," she promised. "Despite the supernatural elements of our lives, we're pretty normal. I think."

"I'll be the judge of that. Now, do you think it's okay if I look at the diaries we found? And what's this about other attics?"

It was as they were going through and seeing how many trunks in the attic belonged to the great-grandmothers that Phillip brought up the neighborhood bash again. "I was thinking about what you said about your father," he said, sitting on the floor surrounded by boxes he had carefully unpacked from Hannah's great-grandmother's trunk. He was currently making a detailed inventory on his phone with all the contents.

Nerd, she thought lovingly.

"Anything specific? My aunt can probably tell you more. She was here pretty much since my father broke the news to her that he was stepping out with a witch."

"I thought you hated that word?"

"We do, but it gets the point across quickly, even if it feels inadequate."

"I definitely want to talk to her when I get the courage." He gave her a boyish grin. "But now..."

His face fell, and she worried what it was that made him worried.

"I know things will change, and I might change my mind later. But for now, I definitely don't want to try to explain this to my family."

She scooted closer to him, reaching out to take his hand in both of hers. "I'm okay with telling whomever you want to tell. I can't guarantee they'll believe any of it, but your family and your friends? They are *still* your family and friends, Phillip. I don't want to take any of that away from you. I'll follow your lead on what to tell them."

"I don't want to see my parents' faces," he admitted. "And they will never believe anything about a curse. They'd be more likely to believe you were slowly poisoning me and I was losing my mind because of it."

Violet laughed as she started to repack the boxes he had completed his inventory on. "I can turn one of them into a toad in front of the other. Would that make them believe in the magic?"

"Can you really?"

"I have never tried, but in theory, yeah." She shrugged. "Never had a reason to turn anyone into a toad before. Faith probably has, I'll bring her along just in case."

She smiled because she knew him, and she knew in his mind he was thinking what it would be like to witness someone turning into a toad.

"I think I might eventually tell my sister," he admitted. "Not right away, not like when I first introduce you. But she is the one I am stuck the most on. I think she can eventually wrap her mind around it. And the two of you, I think, can actually be friends. She deserves to know the truth, and I can't ask you to lie to her forever."

"It would technically only be for ten years," Violet said, trying to lighten the mood. "Besides, we haven't met. She could hate me."

"No, that is pretty much impossible." He shook his head. "I think, no, I know, she will demand to be part of our daughter's life after we're gone, so it seems only fair she knows what that life will be like."

She gently laid the box down in the trunk and twisted back around to face Phillip. "We can tell whomever you want, whenever you want," she promised. "Your family is my family, just as much as my family is yours, now. Which is already complicated." She gestured to the scattered belongings of her cursed predecessors. "And it is going to get slightly more complicated, I fear." She sighed. "I need to talk to my aunt to get an idea on dates, but her son, my cousin, is coming home from the army, and that will make things complicated if he comes here. Which he will, because this is home. We are his family."

"Is this witchy drama or family drama?"

"Everything is mixed together in this family," she said.

"Well, the car made it through." Hannah's voice was audible before her body appeared and joined the other three. "Was it because Violet was there? Because they're together?" Hannah wondered.

Hannah was the appointed lookout to make sure Violet and Phillip made it past the point of the original attack. Invisible to the human eye, she watched Violet drive by with Phillip on Highway 18 before appearing where Patience, Faith, and Abigail were with the remains of Phillip's car in the middle of nowhere.

"That's assuming it was a barrier to keep him from leaving. I don't think that's what this was," Patience said from where she stood in front of Phillip's destroyed car. "There's definitely a central point of impact." She pointed to where it looked like the car had hit a pillar or something right smack in the middle of the hood.

"I always said there was something there," Abigail pointed out from where she had stuck her head through the passenger window.

"Um, hello," Faith said. She gestured to the driver's side where Hannah had ripped the door completely off the frame. "You could just…" Faith mimicked sticking her head in.

"Different perspective," Abigail said, pushing off the door and looking around. "Well, no one else has been here, so your 'stay away' vibes are working."

"You doubt me." Patience rolled her eyes. "Has whatever it was been back, though? Because I doubt my scary vibes would scare this away." She gestured to the damage.

"I don't think so." Abigail shook her head. She looked to Faith, then Hannah. "You sense anything?"

"I never got a good sense of this *thing* the night of," Hannah pointed out. She had been too busy pulling car doors off and stretching the body frame.

"The echoes I felt disappeared before we left the car." Faith shook her head.

"But we seem to mostly be in agreement it was a *thing*, which leaves two questions," Patience said. "What was it, and why now?"

"Violet is going to have her own epiphany tonight," Abigail surprised them.

"She doesn't see the future. None of the rest of us do," Faith pointed out.

"It's not about the future. Not directly. It's a roundabout way of the future. But why?" Abigail wondered, as if asking the car for answers.

The other three shared looks. As used as they were to Abigail having visions, they were still confused.

"Abby." Patience materialized in front of her. "Why *what*?"

"Huh? We need a bloodhound," Abigail said as if it was the simplest solution in the world.

"Like, a real one?"

"I doubt it, but I mean, maybe they can sniff it. This." She gestured to the car. "None of us can. I feel like we're missing something, and I can't find it."

"If you can't, no one can," Hannah said encouragingly.

"A bloodhound could. But there wasn't one before, hmm. No mistake. No bloodhound."

Hannah and Faith shared a look, then looked at Patience, who looked confused but not concerned.

Violet pulled up in front of the three-bed, two-bath home in Palmdale. The neighborhood was exactly as she expected—all single-family homes in the desert with large, albeit brown, yards.

A middle-aged woman opened the door and smiled at Phillip. "You have no idea how good it is to see you after that fright you gave us!" She pulled him into a hug. Despite the fact he was probably eight inches taller, her personality dwarfed him in that moment of embrace.

"Aunt Siobhan, this is Violet," Phillip said.

"These are for you," Violet said, handing her the bouquet that was centered around zinnias. "It is wonderful to meet you."

"These are beautiful. Come in, come in. Phillip, don't be shy showing Violet around. It is not normally this chaotic, but—" she began but was cut off by the scream of children in the backyard. "As you can tell, it is a bit crazy out there."

"I see a bouncy house. That means the best kind of chaos." Violet smiled. "Can I help with anything?"

"Absolutely not. My husband is grilling with the 'help' of the other dads. And I have everything else prepared. Help yourself to food, drinks," Siobhan ordered.

Phillip introduced Violet to his uncle, who came over when he saw him. He grabbed a beer for himself out of the cooler and one of the wine spritzers for Violet when they walked into the backyard.

"My sister, Colleen," he said when Colleen arrived five minutes after them.

"We should have given you a ride. I'm so sorry," Violet said.

"I came up with a friend, who is visiting family, so it all worked out," Colleen said. "Now go away, Phillip, so I can talk about you behind your back."

Violet laughed as Phillip kissed her cheek and went to join his uncle and the other dads around the grill. "I really do feel awful. I forgot you were coming up from LA. We could totally have given you a ride. If you need a ride back or anything..." Violet offered.

"I might. I don't know how long my friend is going to be visiting. I'm glad to finally meet you. I cyber-stalked you, of course. You are amazing at keeping your personal life personal."

"My sisters did the cyberstalking for me on you," Violet admitted. "Do you only do set work? I saw an older website."

"I want to do more, but I haven't done much with the website. It's been mostly word of mouth so far, but it's enough." Colleen smiled.

One of the other neighborhood women came over and joined them, and suddenly, Violet found herself in a circle with all the women.

It was so suburban. So normal.

When the men declared the grilling was done, everyone made up plates.

"Excellent job," Violet teased Phillip when they grabbed seats together.

"I got all of five minutes standing over the grill. I hardly earned any compliments, but I'll take them."

Colleen rolled her eyes as she pulled out her phone to check a text message. "If you can give me a ride back, that'd be great after all."

"Of course," Violet said as they dug into their food.

It was an hour later, and the kids were running around, burning off energy, and they had dragged Phillip over to play with them in what looked possibly like soccer—with some unusual house rules.

"He's great with them." Violet smiled.

"I saw you take a turn in the bounce house," Colleen teased.

Violet laughed. "I haven't seen one in years. It was too tempting."

Colleen nodded, watching Phillip block what looked like a shot into a makeshift goalie, to cheers of half the kids. "But yeah, he is good with kids. Good with everyone, surprisingly, since he loves to hang out in archives and libraries. Once he gets around people, it's like he turns into a golden retriever."

Golden retriever.

Holy shit.

Violet sat straight up in her chair, practically knocking the glass of water she had over.

"Whoa, everything okay?" Colleen asked, concerned.

"Holy shit. Yes, sorry," Violet said and tried to settle back in her chair. "It reminded me of something. A painting I did probably a decade ago. It was such a visceral memory," Violet said slowly, going with a half-truth. Because it was like a kick in the stomach.

What she didn't mention—and now couldn't mention until much later with them carpooling with his sister—was that said painting was done at the behest of her prophetess baby sister. Who, even as a child, didn't do or ask for things without reason.

She couldn't wait to leave.

Phillip hugged his sister when they dropped her off and could finally ask what he had been waiting to ask for the past ninety minutes. "What's going on?"

"Mind if I get us back a little faster?"

"No, is everything okay? Holy shit," he said as they went from being in traffic to being in the garage.

She unbuckled to get out of the car, desperate to start searching. "Something your sister said about how you are a golden retriever. And it's like, of course, you are, and—"

He shot out of the car and turned to look at her. "Hold up. What? No."

Violet grinned as she leaned over the top of her car. "*That's* the part you're tripped on?" She laughed. Her sunglasses were resting on top of her head, framing her hair back, and the hammered gold earrings dangling from her ears jingled as she laughed.

"I'm being mocked by the universe."

"Golden retrievers are adorable. Don't pout, or I can't finish my story."

"All right."

Violet's grin made it clear she was choking back a laugh. "Anyway, the highly accurate statement was like being jolted by electricity. Well, what I imagine it to be like. Suddenly, this memory from like a decade ago came to mind, clear as if it happened yesterday. Of a painting Abigail asked me to paint right after her eighth birthday."

"That's when you get your powers, right?"

Violet nodded. "We refer to it as our 'accession.' How could I have forgotten?" Violet wondered as they reached the door, and Phillip held it open for her.

"Was it like 'Hey, I want this for my birthday?' or 'Hey, baby prophetess here and this is important?'"

"Honestly, at the time, I thought it was the former. And it was a challenge for me because of what she said she wanted it to be. Now I'm beginning to think it's the latter. She has a reason for everything, which is frequently annoying. A fact you'll come to realize soon enough," she promised. "And now I *need* to find this. Well, these. I couldn't fit it on one canvas."

"And you didn't see it in the attic?" He recalled that a few of her paintings were up there, and she had an area dedicated to storage before items sold.

"No, but I wasn't looking for it. And besides, it seems like the universe didn't want me to see it before now. So who knows? Maybe it is up there now."

"That's crazy." He held up his hands in defense when she shot him a poignant look. "Look, I'll accept ocean-splitting powers. I'll even accept the divine—hello, raised Boston Irish Catholic here. But a painting hiding from you for a decade to pop up at this precise moment?"

Violet paused in the middle of the hallway, and he realized they were on their way back up to the attic. He didn't even get distracted by the giant rooms that continued to intimidate him. Maybe he was starting to adjust.

Or it was too dark to see anything. Probably that. Couldn't be intimidated if he couldn't see the rooms filled with Steinway pianos and first edition Jane Austen novels. He didn't want to be intimidated, which he took as progress, but he hadn't stepped foot in half the rooms yet; a fact that overwhelmed him if he thought about it too much.

"Yes," Violet said as she turned to head up.

It took him a minute to remember what he said. That the universe was hiding a painting from her on purpose.

He couldn't come up with a counterargument—yet—so he followed her up.

If nothing else, he relished the chance to look through what was in the attic again. He only had the time to create a detailed inventory for the Exeter line. He felt like he needed permission from the other girls before he went through their family things.

He could tell she hated to admit defeat after over an hour, but it was also near midnight. "If it is the universe, it will have to be revealed," he said, earning a soft smile.

"I might have the wrong attic." Violet sighed.

"Wrong attic? How many do you have? Like, at your aunt's place?"

"Oh, that's a good idea. Maybe I gave it to her? Or my mother did? Hmm," Violet pondered. "No, I was thinking one of the other homes."

"Others?" he choked out. "How many exactly do you have?"

"We only really use this one," she said. "It was more about reclaiming our past."

"Okay. Like buying a home in Swampscott where it all started."

"Not just any home. It's connected to one of the original families. The property, that is. The house has obviously been replaced. I'll ask my aunt in the morning if she's seen it," Violet said.

Chapter Eleven

"You don't have to help. You have to prepare for your classes," Violet said as they appeared in the entranceway of the Swampscott house.

He had seen this house before a couple times, but only this hallway and the living room that opened off it.

"Still time. Although, day after tomorrow is a faculty meeting, and then my adviser is calling for a meeting. I'll be in LA all day."

"Let's see what we find today, then." Violet smiled and led the way up to the attic. "I don't even know what we'll find."

"That's just sad. Is there a system? Like what families or what generations are in each house?"

"Not that I know of, but I never thought about it. Patience will know," Violet determined. "Patience knows everything."

Despite no one living in the home, it was spotless, including the attic. "I took a quick peek when I was here before. There's some things from when we visited growing up."

"Like the Raggedy Andy doll." Phillip laughed and picked it up. He saw the painting she had just finished of a rococo-inspired Raggedy Andy portrait back in the Hollywood home and now knew the setting was this attic with the big box window with a wooden ledge for knick-knacks. "I think I saw one of these at my grandmother's house. Honestly, it kind of creeped me out when I was a kid."

"Don't let him hear you say that," she teased as she pulled it gently from him and tucked him back. "One summer, we forced Faith to marry him. He happened to be the only one we could force into it. Ryan was too old for us to force."

"Ryan?"

"The boy who stayed with us. He left shortly after Hannah's accession. Faith and Abby were both still too young, although Faith was close. How Hannah kept it from him, I don't know, because they were inseparable."

"Fear. Or love," Phillip said. "The two great motivators. Fear of your mothers' wrath?"

"Never. It was mine and Patience's mothers at that time." She looked back down at the doll and smiled at the memory, and yeah, Phillip's heart did a little kick. "It was a beautiful ceremony with tea in the backyard. There are a few Polaroids from it, thanks to *moi*." She gestured to the opposite side of the room. "That over there, though, will have anything older."

"Surely, your painting won't be with the ancestor's stuff," he said. "So we should look on this half of the room."

She closed the gap between them to kiss his cheek. "We can look through the other stuff after," she said. "I'm curious what we have, too."

They found where paintings were stored, but while some of Violet's earliest works were there, no portrait she was looking for.

"Look at this," Phillip said proudly flipping the painting around.

"That should be burned." Violet jumped up, horrified, and tried to snatch it out of his hands.

He held it above his head. While Violet was tall, she still couldn't reach it up there. "It's cute." And it was. He couldn't explain it because, yeah, the painting was awful in the way first paintings were for people. But something about it spoke to her as a child, he could practically see a young girl painting this in the backyard or on the beach. And since he knew what she looked like as a child, thanks to their spelunking adventures in the Hollywood home, he could easily see a young Violet painting this.

"It's *awful*. I was still learning figures, and that horse is shorter in length than the person is tall!"

"It's adorable. If only there was a portrait of a young girl painting said picture."

"Just you wait," Violet said. "Well, it's not here. I didn't see it in any of the rooms downstairs when I checked on the house over the summer. Want to look through the old stuff?"

"Hell yes. But gently. Preferably with gloves."

Violet laughed as she went to one side of a trunk. He was on the other side so they could pull it away from the wall.

"Well, luck of the draw, and the first one is from my family," Violet said as she saw the stylized *E* on the lid.

"*E* could stand for Eliza, or Elsbeth, or Emily. Not necessarily Exeter," he said. "Let's not jump to conclusions."

"Yes, sir," she teased with a flimsy salute as she sat cross-legged before it. "Honestly, I don't know what we'll find. This is exciting!"

"Did you spend a lot of time here?"

"Not really. I remember my first white Christmas was here. I think it was the year Abigail was born, and we lost her mother. She was just an infant. A summer vacation now and again. Which is why I thought it had to be here because I would have completely forgotten about it. It was years since I was here last before this summer."

"Thank God you came this summer."

Violet laughed as she gently pulled out a box filled with something heavy. Opening it, she found a diary. "Did I tell you about why I was in Swampscott?"

"Abigail had a dream. Which sounds insane when you say it out loud. *Is that a diary?*" He realized what she was holding.

Violet gently fingered the leather cover. It showed signs of wear from sitting in a box in a trunk for however many years but overall seemed to be fine. She gently opened the cover—mostly because she was worried she'd give Phillip heart palpitations for handling it barehanded and daring to read it.

"I can't tell if you're salivating because you're excited or going to have a heart attack. Give a girl some warning on the latter in case I need to bring in back up."

"So I'm not invincible after you all healed me?"

"Well, Abigail did most of the healing, with some help from me, but no. The curse is what makes you invincible, but that doesn't mean you can't get hurt. It means it won't kill you, but the process of healing can take time and be a bitch. We just sped it up the other day."

He brushed her hair back to steal a kiss. He knew the topic of the curse hurt her to bring up. He could see the guilt on her face. "There are so many questions, so many things I am going to love learning about you over the next ten years," he promised. "Starting with if you are going to share that treasure with me or make me beg."

She laughed as he'd hoped and pulled him down to sit next to her. "I'll be nice and share. I feel bad about destroying the letter at the archives."

"Couldn't even leave me crumbs."

"One piece of paper is hardly enough to do your dissertation on," she pointed out. "Have to keep all the other nerdy hot graduate students from discovering it."

"Fair point."

Violet gently reopened the diary and gasped. "It's older than it looks. It says Geranium Exeter. Oh my God. Holy shit!"

"Who is Geranium? Wait, are your ancestors all named after flowers?"

"Since the first—the first with the curse at least. Hyacinth was the one murdered in the witch trials. Her daughter, the first of us with this curse, was Geranium."

"You mean to tell me you have a *three-hundred*-year-old diary causally tossed in a shoe box in a trunk in an attic without climate control?"

"Heart palpitations?" she asked.

He nodded.

"In my defense, I had no idea this even existed. I have my mother's diary, her mother's. I have six generations back home. Would you like to read them?"

He rested his head in his hands, and she laughed before shoving him over.

"You are forgetting one very important factor, darling." Violet smiled. She placed her index finger on the now-closed journal, and the aging and other damage faded away.

"Better," he said as he rubbed his chest. "Damn it, all these journals now when I need to prep for work. I'd rather be reading."

She leaned over to kiss his cheek. Never in a million years did she think she'd fall for a bookworm.

"You have ten years," she reminded him. "We'll find even more for you. If there's one, there has to be more."

Chapter Twelve

It was almost a mimic of life before Phillip: Hannah played a repertoire of Chopin on the piano while Violet read from one of the couches. Hannah cherished the moment; she loved that Violet found someone but a small part of her feared what it signaled. That the curse was in full swing for all of them. A ridiculous thought since the curse had its claws in them from the moment they were born.

"No Phillip today?" Patience asked as she walked in on them.

"He's prepping for the beginning of the school year. He wants to make progress before his meeting tomorrow with the other faculty and principal."

"Have you seen the journal?" Hannah asked over the music.

"Journal?" Patience's eyebrows scrunched together.

"We found it while looking for something else. Geranium Exeter's journal." Violet held it up. "Knowing how it ends is heartbreaking because she has no idea. She's just living her life, mourning a mother she never knew, falling in love. The normal things until..."

She didn't need to continue, they all knew. Until the Neapolis daughter died at 24, followed by the Orleans daughter. Was it better to not know? Not spend a whole life waiting for someone to die?

Patience's voice cut into Hannah's introspection. "What were you looking for in Swampscott?"

"Wait, you knew about the journal?" Violet asked, surprised, sitting up straight to look at the eldest girl.

"I'm not surprised. There is a trunk for each family in the attic. I don't recall all the things inside, but I remember Aunt Isabel pulled out some things, including diaries," Patience said, naming Hannah's mother.

"And you never said?"

"You never asked. I didn't even know you were looking for something. I still don't know what you're looking for," Patience pointed out.

"A painting, well, a set, because I couldn't fit it on one canvas. From like a decade ago. What else is in the attic? Do you mind if Phillip reads the diaries you have? I said he could read the ones I have from the Exeter line. Hannah is okay with him reading the Milan line's."

"Except for my own." Hannah smirked as she continued to play.

"Of course. I'll see which ones we have. I believe I have a complete set. But like this one," she jerked her thumb towards Hannah, "I'll keep my own under lock and key."

"Of course." Violet glanced over at Hannah and rolled her eyes. Just like a Dubrovnik to have everything neatly organized.

"What paintings?"

"The one Abigail asked me to make, right after her accession."

"They're in Galveston," Patience said. "I believe one is hanging in a bedroom, and the other is in the sitting room."

"Really? I have to tell Phillip. Wait, let me check they're there before I drag him away from work." Violet disappeared with the journal gently set on the couch.

"She doesn't realize it," Hannah said as she paused in her playing. 'It' being how the dynamics were already changing. It wasn't a surprise but it was weird, bringing in an outsider.

"There's nothing to realize," Patience said with a defeated shrug. "It was going to happen. It will happen for you if you want it to," Patience said. "Things change. We knew it would. There was no way Violet was going to be alone. When is your workshop?"

"Two weeks. Thanks for letting me move back in."

"It's your home, Hannah. Although maybe don't bitch too much about dorm life in front of Rose and Abigail. Rose needs to be out on her own. Try nudging Abby. Maybe if we team up on her." Patience smiled as she picked up the diary and set it gently on the bookshelf. No risk of anyone accidentally knocking it around or knocking something on top of it. "Don't say anything to Vi."

"For what it's worth, Patience. I don't know if I'll find what I want. What I do know is you don't deserve it." The curse. Being alone.

"The universe doesn't care what we deserve. And my break is over. I have a call to make," Patience said, checking her watch to see the time.

Hannah went back to playing but couldn't help but shake her head. Her fingers never missed a key, but her head—and most certainly her heart—weren't in the music any longer.

The family dynamics were changing, and for the first time in a while, Hannah felt the curse closing in. Whether eight years—the time she had left—was enough, she didn't know.

"Where the hell are you?"

Phillip opened the door, surprised to see Violet on his doorstep. "Hey!" They hadn't mentioned meeting up, and now that his meetings were over, he definitely just wanted to crash—preferably with Violet. "Are you a mind reader?"

Her laughter filtered through him and washed away the worse of the stress and exhaustion. She held up a bag. "I brought food. I figured you would be too tired to cook."

"Bold assumption I cook, period. That's what the microwave is for."

"Is that because you're a guy or because you're a grad student?" she asked.

"The latter. Here." He took the bag from her as she came in. "Pinks?" It was a Los Angeles institution he quickly learned to love when he moved to LA.

"Who doesn't like Pinks? I had a vague memory you said you liked your hotdog with mustard and relish. I hope that's right."

He leaned in to kiss her as he closed the door. "It's perfect. What brings you by?"

"You had two important meetings today. I wanted to see how you were, and how the meetings went. Do you have plates? Like, real plates?"

"Believe it or not, yes. Probably even two."

She laughed as she followed him to the kitchen. It was the size of a shoebox. He could stretch out his arms and touch both walls, and you had to stand on the side when opening the refrigerator or you wouldn't be able to open it completely.

"I'll wait out here," she teased, not crossing into the kitchen. "You're forgiven for not cooking. I'm not sure two people will fit in there."

"You should have seen my apartment in Boston. It really was a one-butt kitchen, as my sister called it. One sink, no dishwasher, no garbage disposal, and the fridge was half this size."

"How did the meetings go?" she asked, moving to sit on the floor in front of his coffee table once she took the plates from him. She split the food between the two of them.

"The surrealness of the job is gone. With classes starting next week, it really drove home how much I have to do in the next week."

"Like what? I went to high school, so did Patience." Implying she had an idea of what it was like.

"Your other sisters didn't?" There was so much he had to learn still, and he was sure if they had a hundred years together, he would always find some new, fascinating thing about her.

"We all get pulled out of school when we come into our powers. Too risky since we were eight. Faith would definitely have used them to punish anyone that annoyed her." Violet grinned before biting into the hot dog. "Faith still punishes people who annoy her."

"But you and Patience went back in high school? That must have been rough, being that old."

"My cousin was there and was only one year older than Patience, so she had someone looking out for her. Neither of us particularly cared for it, but we survived. This is about you," she redirected.

"I talked with the other history teachers—there's two—and went over what I have so far on my syllabi. They both said, one way or another, that I was a typical first-year teacher and would quickly find my lesson plans are wishful thinking."

"Better to overprepare than under!"

He grinned as he opened the second hot dog. "My thoughts."

"What about with your adviser?"

"She's sympathetic but said in no uncertain words that if I don't find something, I need to pivot. We talked about what I could do, but I haven't found anything that I particularly like yet. Since I'm working full time, they're putting my status as graduate student on hold at least this semester so that I don't have to pay the fees while I think about it."

"That's nice of them."

"I forget the fancy terminology, but basically, I should still be able to access the libraries."

"If they don't let you, you could ask Rose. She's starting in the fall, and Faith's in her second year."

"Wait, both at UCLA?" he asked, surprised. "I knew Faith was on the beach volleyball team."

"Rose is starting, wanting to get the bachelor's in nursing. We're insisting she gets her own apartment or lives on campus. Patience and I want her to have those normal experiences. Including dorm life."

"What about Abigail? She's the same age as Rose, I thought."

"A couple months younger, but yes, she could go to college. She doesn't know what she wants to do. Besides, I wanted to talk about you."

He studied her as they split the fries. He pointed his fry at her. "What's going on?"

"We've been doing so much about *my* family. We haven't focused on you. And that's not right or fair. You have all this coming on."

"High school teacher versus cursed family. One is *definitely* much more interesting, and I'll tell you it isn't high school. Although high school may be more toxic than this generational curse."

She laughed as she waved a hand. Their trash disappeared, and the plates cleaned. "I'm new to this, I know. So if I am being unbalanced in our relationship, tell me, Phillip. Nothing makes up for the curse, but I want our time together to be one of partners. The curse dictates so much as it is."

He pulled her up onto the couch next to him. "I'm not joking when I say the curse is much more interesting than this." He gestured widely. "I'm a big boy. I promise to speak up."

"What were some of the ideas your adviser had? Still witch trials related?"

"Nothing that speaks to me. So instead, I'm going to spend the weekend finishing up the lesson plans for next month—I don't care what the others say. The principal wants them a month in advance, and I'm too new to contradict her so she'll have them a month in advance. Then I can read your ancestors' journals."

"I have something to show you, but it will wait till tomorrow. Not about the paintings. Patience has all of her ancestors' journals, of course, and is happy to let you read them too."

"*That* is the best news today!"

"I still can't believe you didn't tell me yesterday." Phillip pretended to pout as they stood in the Galveston, Texas house in front of one of the portraits. This one happened to have four dogs clearly paused in playing with each other. It was set outside but nothing specific to give it a location.

"It was important to me that yesterday was about you," Violet explained, again. She had the realization when Patience told her where the paintings were that she instantly wanted to go grab Phillip to get them, and she realized that meant making him drop everything to do this thing for her. His stuff had to be just as important as hers.

"Not a *hint*," he teased.

"If I told you, you would demand we went last night, and I liked making yesterday about you instead." She smiled. "Okay, let's see if the other is in a bedroom like Patience said."

"*Third* house," he mumbled. "What's the history here?"

"Last place the sisters lived before moving to California. I'm going to guess they got tired of hurricanes."

"This house would not have been damaged by those," Phillip guessed.

"No, but they decided to try further out west. Because unpredictable earthquakes were preferred to predictable hurricanes." Violet shook her head. The first floor had one guest room but no painting.

"So what do you do with the house? Leave it like in Swampscott?"

"Pretty much. I think Patience has an idea of renting it out during tourist season. Our mothers did that when we were younger, but we haven't."

It was the last bedroom they came to, of course, but there it was, casually hanging on the wall as if to say, *I've been here all along, dummy.*

"I feel judged by a painting," Phillip decided, making her laugh.

"Now who is the mind reader?" she mused. She went to take it off the wall, and they went back downstairs to grab the other.

"No secret message on the back?" Phillip asked and flipped them around. "One could hope." He sighed, seeing the blank backs. "Maybe ultraviolet light."

"This isn't some heist movie." Violet rolled her eyes, and a heartbeat later, they were back in her bedroom with the paintings.

"Well, what does it speak to you, then?" Phillip asked and held up the second portrait.

This one had three dogs sharing the space comfortably, not really playing or interacting but not ignoring the others. A golden retriever, a Belgian Malinois, and a mutt.

"Well?"

"Let's find Abby. She wanted them painted," Violet said.

They only brought the one with three dogs with them, and it took all of three minutes to find Abigail coming out of her room to head downstairs.

"Look what I found!" Violet said triumphantly as she and Phillip cornered Abigail.

"Um, congratulations?" Abigail asked, her eyebrows drawing together.

"Don't you recognize it?"

"Am I supposed to?"

"You told me to paint it!"

"Wait, I did?" Abigail asked, her ice-blue eyes wide in surprise, leaning in to study the painting more closely. "Why?"

"Oh my sweet heavens." Violet shook the painting at her in frustration. "How am I supposed to know? You're the one with the visions! Why?"

"Wait, do you not remember all of your visions?" Phillip asked.

"Clearly not. It's a cute painting, though," Abigail said. "How long ago?"

"You were eight."

"That was ten years ago!" Abigail pointed out. "How am I supposed to remember? What did I say?"

"I don't remember the exact language, but you wanted me to paint specific dog breeds."

"Huh, interesting," Abigail said, taking another look at the painting. "Why a golden retriever, a mutt, and— Is that a Belgian Malinois? Did I even know what that was when I was eight?"

"Apparently, it was what you told me."

"You did great work." Abigail gave her two thumbs up. "Off to look at cars with Faith," she added as she turned to walk out. She gave them a look right before exiting. "Where's the other half?"

Phillip laughed as Violet mimed throwing the painting at her sister. He took the painting out of her hands with one hand, the other grabbing her waist to pull her close, and kissed her cheek.

"How much of that was bratty little sister?"

"Who knows?" Violet threw her hands up. "I give up!"

"Give up on what?" Patience asked, walking through.

"There are days I would murder Abby if it was possible."

"What did she do now?"

"She asked me to paint this." Violet took it from Phillip's hand and turned it for Patience to see.

"You finally found them, then."

"Why do we have so many attics?" Violet demanded.

"Because we have three hundred years' worth of memories?" Patience shrugged. An alarm went off on her phone, and she left them in the hallway, too.

"You can't murder your sisters," Phillip said when Violet turned to him.

"Are you sure? I mean, they wouldn't stay dead," Violet pointed out. "Let's grab the other one and see if we can force anything out of them."

"Abby was mad I didn't paint them all in one. But I didn't know all the breeds well, so I had to study them. But she said that I broke them up correctly. Whatever that means." Violet sighed.

"Well, do a golden retriever, Belgian Malinois, and mutt have anything in common?" Phillip asked, looking at the portrait of three.

"Other than being dogs? Nothing that I know of."

Phillip turned to the second painting. "Well, you have a German shepherd, blue pit bull, Doberman, and Great Pyrenees."

"Good eye." Violet smiled. "And again, all dogs. That's the extent of my knowledge."

"You're the artist," he pointed out. "Not only of these, I mean, in general. So what do we look for? Assuming we look for anything and they're not just nice paintings of dogs."

"I mean...they could be," Violet hedged. "It could just have been a memory was unlocked in that conversation, nothing more."

"What about that conversation made you think of it? I mean, maybe there was something specific you reacted to. That could be a clue."

Violet blushed, making Phillip smile. "Did I make you blush? Over what?"

"I'll plead the fifth. On all of it."

"So we'll hang these up and look at them every day. They are really nice paintings. Did you ever have a dog?" he asked.

"No. I mean, not really. There was enough death when we were growing up, so we never had any pets. They die, too. But when I go with Auntie to visit family on the reservation or go to friends, they have dogs. We actually fostered for a while, so we had temporary dogs. And cats. And once a pig."

"A pig."

"Long story," Violet grinned. "We haven't fostered in a while. I don't know why."

"Well, I think they'd look good here," Phillip said as he gestured to the wall opposite her bed. "We can wake up and see them every morning. And before bed."

"What are you getting at?" She raised an eyebrow.

"I'm new to all this, I know, so I could be completely wrong. But I don't think it was just unlocking a memory. Or rather, I don't think that's all it was. Your reaction was too big. Your drive to find these was too big. So there should be a reason."

"New, but brilliant at all this." Violet walked over to pick up the painting with three dogs. "You have to promise not to laugh. Or get offended."

"I don't know which will be harder."

She smiled and then gently tapped the golden retriever. "You."

"What?"

"It's you."

"I'm a dog?"

Violet laughed. "Yes. You are such a golden retriever type."

"Wait, this again? Is that good? I feel like I should have a say in this."

She laughed as she hung the painting on the wall with a zap of magic where he had originally pointed. It made it easier for them to both stand and look at it and see both paintings together as they were intended.

"You were playing with your nieces and nephew, their friends, and your sister came up. I was admiring how great you were with them—and how adorable." She grinned and noticed the slightest blush to his cheek, which made her want to lean up and kiss it, so she did just that. She had a lifetime of affection to give in the next ten years. "Your sister said something about how you were totally a golden retriever type, and it was like a kick in the stomach."

"Okay, we'll circle back to that because I'm not upset but have questions. So if this is like the Rosetta Stone and this is some sort of message, I'm like the first key to decoding it."

"Holy shit."

"What? What did I say?"

"No, continue the thought."

"Well, there wasn't that much more. That would be me, then." He pointed to the golden. "That's all I got at the moment. What did I say?"

"Remember how I went to Swampscott because Abigail had a dream?"

He nodded.

"She said I was looking for a key to open my lock. I know it was all metaphors, but you are the key. My key." She blushed. "I intentionally was blind to it and looking for a physical lock, and once you start looking, there are locks everywhere. Which led to breaking into museums at night to see if they were the right ones. And then I saw your damn tattoo," she trailed off.

"I don't think a decade is long enough to catch up on all the stories you have." Phillip grinned. "Hey." He pulled her close and tipped up her chin. "I'm the lucky one. Other than going back to high school. If I absolutely hate it, I may volunteer to be a house husband."

She laughed and knew he was trying to soothe her because every time she thought about him dying—him dying *because* of her—it made her sick to her stomach.

"We are either completely off base and it is simply a portrait of dogs," Violet finally spoke up, "or there's something in there because a psychic told me to paint it and you are the key to beginning to unravel its meaning."

"I'm leaning toward option number two because nothing with you is ordinary. And even if Abigail doesn't remember asking you to paint it—"

"If," Violet practically snarled, making Phillip laugh as he held her wrapped in his arms.

"She still asked you to paint it for some reason."

"Probably. I agree. Option two seems more likely, given all the actors involved. Maybe we can prompt her to remember," Violet said thoughtfully, leaning her head against his shoulder with the top of her head tucking right at the bottom his chin. "We honestly don't know how it works for her. She may know and not share all of the rules with us. But I do know she can go looking for visions, and if she had a vision once about this, she can at least remember it somehow."

"Would you have painted any clues into the painting?"

"Anything she told me at the time, but I don't remember anything." She took a step forward and studied it closely. "I feel like it's our backyard. Not exact, but definitely inspired by. For both of them," she said, looking closely. "Whether that was because it was what I was looking at that summer or some other reason, who knows?"

"Do you normally paint in things? Hidden symbols, an object that crops up a lot, anything like that?"

She gave him a look. "Do I look like I'm leaving clues for treasure hunters or something?" She put her face close to see if there was a small detail she had missed. "There's something on the collar." Violet pointed to the Malinois. "Do you see it?"

"It looks like a patch."

"Hmm, I know I didn't do that, and I don't know what it's for." Violet sighed. She heard music coming from the music room, so she grabbed one painting. Phillip grabbed the other, and they went downstairs.

When Hannah finished the piece, she looked up at them.

"Quick question, and we'll leave you be," Violet said. "I remembered these from ages ago, found them. Do you remember them?"

"I mean, I think I remember you painting in the backyard now that I'm looking at them. Why?"

"Trying to figure out something. Does anything jump out at you? From inside the painting, I mean?"

Hannah looked at both of them, even standing to come look more closely. "I like them, but no, nothing jumps out at me. Was there something specific you wanted me to see?"

"No, just trying to see what jumps out at people," Violet said. "Remember how I told you Phillip's sister is a set photographer?"

"Yeah, have our paths crossed?"

"Probably not, but the way things are going now, you probably will." Violet smiled. "Get back to playing. Thanks for helping."

"Happy to."

When it was just them, Phillip asked, "Most people would say 'keep practicing' but you said playing."

"Music comes as naturally to Hannah as breathing air. Hers is one brain I wouldn't mind getting into for a day. She hears something, and she can play it back. She sight-reads. She learned the piano as a child, then decided to learn the cello to challenge herself. I think she entertained the idea of learning the harp just so she could play it in historical movies for fun."

In the end, none of her sisters were of any help. Something she pointed out to each of them.

Chapter Thirteen

Her cousin found her the next day while she painted in her studio. Phillip was finishing up his lesson plans at the desk she used more for catching items than anything else.

"Am I interrupting?" Rose asked.

Violet shook her head. "I think I'm nearly done with this commission. We'll see if the customer agrees," she said and put her paints down. "What's up?"

"I didn't want to say yesterday in front of everyone, especially Patience, but I had an idea on the painting."

That caught Phillip's attention, and his head snapped up. "Should I leave?"

"No, please, this includes you," Rose said quickly. "You know how you said you thought the golden retriever was Phillip?" She waited for Violet to nod. "Can you bring that one of the three down?"

A moment later, the painting appeared on an easel in front of them. "I'm not sure. It's probably because I'm thinking of him, but this one." She pointed to the

Belgian Malinois. "The thing on his collar? It reminds me of the badge for the military. And Malinois are often used in the military."

Violet sucked in her breath, seeing where her cousin was going. "I never painted that on its collar," Violet said.

"And you don't think Abigail couldn't go in and add a little detail later?" Rose pointed out with a knowing look.

"Wait. Civilian here," Phillip reminded them.

"I think the Malinois represents my brother," Rose said. "He joined the army the day after he graduated high school and has been serving since. His contract is ending, and he's coming home," Rose said happily. "But if one dog represents a person, what's to say they don't all?"

"That's genius," Phillip pointed out. "If I'm a golden retriever—still not sold on that."

Violet shared an amused look with her cousin. Even in their short time knowing him, they all agreed Phillip was a golden retriever type.

"Just something, but I didn't want to speak in front of Patience," Rose said. "Anyway, Abby and Faith are taking me shopping for my dorm."

Phillip waited for Rose to leave before asking, "Why are we not mentioning your cousin in front of Patience?"

"The short version is he was part of her curse. He broke her heart," Violet said. She'd tell him the whole story when she was guaranteed privacy.

"Okay, if we go with this idea of the dogs representing people, which I like the more I think about it, that leaves a lot of questions," Phillip said.

Violet nodded in agreement. "Who are the others, and why did I break them into these two groups? At the time, I thought it was because I didn't have the correct size canvas, but now, I'm not so sure. I could have made them smaller. I could have split them into different groups. So there's meaning in that, too."

Violet gave the painting another thorough look. "The background is the same. I know it's not any particular place, but at least in the paintings, it is the same place."

She studied the painting with a frown. "You're here. He's coming home. Does that mean the place is here?" Violet wondered.

"Who is the third man in your life?" he asked, Violet's jaw dropping. Phillip smiled gently. "If that is me, and that is your cousin, then one line of inquiry is we're both connected to you so the third dog-slash-metaphorical-person is also connected to you somehow."

Violet looked between him and the painting. "That doesn't feel right. The only other man was my father, but he's passed. The three of you will certainly never be out in the yard together. Maybe... Abigail said when she told me about her dream, about my lock, that she thought things were changing but never elaborated on that."

Things were definitely changing for the family with Phillip joining them. That wasn't new. There were at least two men in every generation that Violet was aware of. Abigail's talk of change seemed way too sinister to be about men joining the family. Before she could ask him if he thought the mutt could possibly be the next guy to join the family sometime in the future, Phillip cleared his throat.

"About Abby."

Violet snapped her head around, curious. "What about her?"

"The first dinner. Her list of answers before I asked questions? Remember how she said I had an epiphany?" He waited for Violet to nod before continuing. "She gave more answers than questions, it seemed."

"You had your own revelation," Violet remembered. "Abby picked up on that. You didn't share."

"I figured it was something everyone else knew, so I kept it to myself. I thought she gave more answers than questions. That's because I misinterpreted her. 'Sometimes' and 'only on Fridays' were part of the same answer. It seems like a little thing, I know, and is definitely something you already knew having grown up together. But it's giving me pause whenever Abigail says anything now, waiting a beat and trying to decide if what I hear is what she says. That makes no sense," he leaned back to sit on top of the desk. "I guess what I'm trying to say is I'm seeing how Abigail cannot be taken at her word. She means everything she says, but we don't have all the information we need to decode what she says."

"I told you, you are good at this." Violet smiled. "Which, if things are changing, might be a blessing for us."

Both of their phones received a text at the same time.

Everyone else responded quickly with their names for Phillip, from Abigail to Maxine, so he could save their contact info.

"Welcome to the family group chat." Violet smiled. "I'm going to start on a new commission. Want to walk me through your lesson plans?" she asked as she pulled out a clean canvas.

"I know I'm getting ahead of myself, and I may not even like teaching... But I know the person who currently teaches the honor classes is retiring in a couple years, and I would love to have those classes, I think," Phillip said thoughtfully as he resumed his seat. "Why am I still talking like I'll be teaching high school? Even after I finish the dissertation?"

She grinned at his horrified tone. Her back was to him as she prepped her canvas. She wasn't the psychic and had no idea if he would like teaching high school or not, but what she did know, what made her heart soar, was this moment. Everything was so domestic, so perfect.

She remembered her aunt's words from the night of Phillip's accident, and it brought a sense of calm and a tinge of joy. Yes, she was her mother's daughter and inherited her sense of fairness as well as a generational curse. She focused on that so much the last few years as the curse seemed to breathe down all their necks, racing to the first of their generation to die.

She couldn't bear to think of a world where she had to bury her sisters, yet that was coming too quickly. Instead, she decided to focus on the other advice her aunt gave her that night.

She was her father's daughter, too, and would love fiercely with no regrets.

Emma Jo Gregory is a pen name and alter ego of a college professor (shhh). By day she researches *very* different matters, by night (and weekends) she escapes into alternate realities. A native of Southern California she now finds herself in Texas enjoying the food but not the humidity, thank you very much.

Emma has made up tales since she was a child, subjecting her younger sisters as her first audience. They continue to be her biggest critics (and support group), which is why you'll probably see themes of sisterhood and family in all her writing. You can follow Emma Jo on instagram, facebook, or her monthly newsletter at emmajogregory.substack.com